"I still can't believe you don't decorate for Christmas," Miranda said.

Simon held Hudson and Harper in his lap while she put a green hat on Hudson. His little Santa's-helper suit and Harper's matching female elf would go nicely with Zig and Zag, the dogs Miranda adorably still thought of as twins.

"What would be the point? It's only me and the dogs, and they don't care that it's Christmas."

"Hello—Christmas spirit, where are you? What happened to getting in the mood for all things merry and bright?"

Simon snorted. "When have you ever known me to be merry and bright?"

But sitting here cross-legged with both of the twins on his lap and Miranda zipping around with unflagging energy and excitement, he thought he might be as close as he'd ever been to those feelings.

There was just something right about the four of them being here together. He wanted to tell her. But the words wouldn't come. They got all tangled up in his head and never made it to his lips.

Publishers Weekly bestselling and award-winning author **Deb Kastner** writes stories of faith, family and community in a small-town Western setting. She lives in Colorado with her husband and a pack of miscreant mutts, and is blessed with three daughters and two grandchildren. She enjoys spoiling her grandkids, movies, music (The Texas Tenors!), singing in the church choir and exploring Colorado on horseback.

Books by Deb Kastner

Love Inspired

Christmas Twins

Texas Christmas Twins

Cowboy Country

Yuletide Baby
The Cowboy's Forever Family
The Cowboy's Surprise Baby
The Cowboy's Twins
Mistletoe Daddy
The Cowboy's Baby Blessing

Email Order Brides

Phoebe's Groom
The Doctor's Secret Son
The Nanny's Twin Blessings
Meeting Mr. Right

Visit the Author Profile page at Harlequin.com for more titles.

Texas
Christmas Twins

Deb Kastner

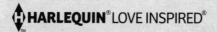

HARLEQUIN® LOVE INSPIRED®

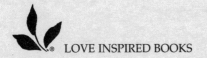

Recycling programs for this product may not exist in your area.

LOVE INSPIRED BOOKS

ISBN-13: 978-0-373-89968-5

Texas Christmas Twins

Copyright © 2017 by Debra Kastner

www.Harlequin.com

Printed in U.S.A.

Through Him then let us continually offer God a sacrifice of praise, that is, the fruit of lips that confess His name. Do not neglect to do good and to share what you have; God is pleased by sacrifices of that kind.

—*Hebrews* 13:15–16

What can I give Him, poor that I am?
If I were a shepherd, I would bring a lamb.
If I were a Wise Man, I would do my part.
Yet what I can I give Him: give my heart.

Chapter One

Miranda Morgan wouldn't even know what hit her.

He was here in front of her cabin, preparing to make certain of that. After he was through with her, the powers that be would want to name a tempest after him.

Hurricane Simon.

It didn't matter that he hadn't seen Miranda since high school, or even, as his best friend Mason's kid sister, that she'd bared the occasional brunt of his pranks and mean jokes. In another situation, he might be considering how to make amends and not additional strife. He was a new man, a man of faith. The Lord had changed his heart, and now Simon's goal was to change his life to match what had happened internally.

But try as he might, he fell short of being able to forgive Miranda for ignoring her responsibility to the sweet nine-month-old twins now in her care.

If this was a spiritual test, a trial in his bumpy new Christian life, it was a doozy.

Miranda was an eminently successful celebrity photographer. But he couldn't care less about movie stars and the la-di-da lifestyles of the rich and famous. He was a simple ranch owner and dog trainer and he liked his solitary country life.

What he *didn't* like was Miranda. She couldn't even be bothered to fly home to Texas long enough to attend her own twin niece's and nephew's christening, and she was not only Hudson and Harper's aunt, but had also been named their godmother.

And yet she hadn't managed to spare even one weekend for them.

Even Simon had been in church that day, though at the time he hadn't been a churchgoing man. He remembered feeling uncomfortable, but he'd *been there*. Simon was the twins' godfather, and to him, it was a big thing, a sacred duty, a promise that he'd always be there for Hudson and Harper in any way they needed.

Obviously, Miranda didn't feel the same way. Family obligations clearly meant nothing to her.

And now, through a cruel twist of fate, Miranda had been named the twins' permanent legal guardian.

How could that even *be*? The very thought of it was both confusing and infuriating.

It was painful enough that Mary, Mason's youngest sister, and her husband, John, had been taken from this world prematurely by the merciless act of a drunkard who'd made the deadly choice to drive while intoxicated.

But for Mary to name self-serving, high-flying *Miranda* as the twins' legal guardian, even after all she had done, or *not* done, for Mary and the babies—

Well, that made less sense than putting a Border collie in a room full of cats and expecting him to herd them.

What had Mary been thinking? How could she have considered her sister a worthwhile guardian, one with whom she could entrust innocent children? What kind of mother would a woman like Miranda possibly be?

Inconceivable.

Why hadn't Mason and his wife, Charlotte, been named the twins' guardians? They already had four children of their own with a fifth on the way. They were wonderful, experienced parents who *had* been there for Mary and the twins during every stage of their lives.

Mary might have sincerely believed that two more children would have been too much of a burden on Mason and Charlotte, and that they had their own family to think of and provide for.

But choosing *Miranda*?

Mary might have been sincere, but she'd been sincerely *wrong*.

However the future played out now that Miranda was the twins' legal guardian, Simon's determination to be a positive influence in his godchildren's lives hadn't changed one iota. They had always been a priority with him, but even more so now.

If Miranda was anything like Simon imagined her to be, Harper and Hudson would need all the protection and stability they could get.

He was going to step up for those two precious babies.

Unfortunately, that also meant he would, by default, be in contact with Miranda. She would have to let him into her world, whether she liked it or not. And likewise, he'd have to learn to work with her. They didn't have to be friends, but they would have to get along.

For the twins' sakes, he reminded himself as he removed his brown Stetson, combed his fingers back through his thick blond hair and knocked on the door.

"It's open" he heard Miranda call from somewhere inside the cabin, her voice muffled and distant.

Feeling awkward at having to let himself into a cabin he was unfamiliar with, he opened the door and stepped inside. He didn't immediately see Miranda, or the twins, either, for that matter.

His attention was instead captured by the insane display of Christmas decorations, red and green, silver and gold, everywhere his gaze landed.

It looked as if the North Pole had exploded in her living room.

An enormous eight-foot Christmas tree stood in one corner, the flashing angel topper just barely clearing the ceiling. Presents wrapped in colorful aluminum paper were piled high underneath the tree.

She'd arranged a large Nativity set, complete with a stable and an angel proclaiming Peace on Earth, on the end table.

Shiny red and gold garland adorned every wall, with evergreen garland gracing the fireplace where the stockings were hung with care, as the poem went. *Homemade* stockings, with Hudson and Harper's names written in flourishes of red and green glitter glue.

This woman was clearly obsessed with Christmas.

And apparently, shiny things.

It took him a moment to focus and find Miranda. He supposed he'd expected to find her changing a diaper or two, or feeding the twins their bottles—or whatever it was that nine-month-old babies ate—as the reason she couldn't answer the door. Instead, she was right there in the middle of the living room, stretched out on her stomach underneath a card table that she'd draped with sheets, holding a flashlight she was beaming on a picture book as Harper and Hudson cuddled on either side of her.

Of all the crazy, unexpected scenarios, this one took the cake.

Or the Christmas *fruitcake* as the case might be.

The tent was ingenious. She'd used stacks of hardback books to fasten the edges of the sheet to the sofa on one side of them and an armchair on the other, with the card table holding up the structure in the middle.

Lying on her stomach, jammed under a table only a few feet high, couldn't possibly be comfortable for her, with her tall, lithe frame, and yet she had an enthusiastic smile on her face and didn't look the least bit put out by the awkward position. He suspected her feet might be protruding out the back, although he couldn't confirm that from his current vantage point.

She shined the flashlight at his face, momentarily blinding him, and he held up a hand to block the light.

"Simon?" she questioned, surprise lining her tone. "Simon West?"

He was astonished she recognized him. He'd added a few inches to his frame in the years since they'd seen each other last, not to mention a few pounds. He'd stayed at the outskirts of John and Mary's funeral and hadn't spoken to anyone but Mason and Charlotte.

"*Uncle* Simon," he corrected her tersely, nodding toward the twins. "It's an honorary title."

Of which he was very, very proud.

"Well, *Uncle Simon*, you're more than welcome to join us." She shifted herself and the twins to the side to make room for him in the tiny strung-up tent.

"I'm welcome to—" he repeated. He'd walked into her house out of the blue. She had no idea why he was here, and yet she'd immediately offered him the opportunity to join in their…*adventure*.

"What are you doing here, by the way?" she asked curiously.

"I—er—"

Her offer completely threw him off his game, and for a moment he was fairly certain he was gaping and couldn't remember his own name, much less why he had come.

Eventually, he shook his head. There was no way he was going to get his large frame under that small table, no matter how hard he squeezed. And honestly, he didn't even really want to try.

"We can make it work," Miranda insisted, clearly not taking no for an answer. "I'm sure the twins will love spending quality time with their uncle Simon."

She couldn't possibly know it, but she'd just touched on his weak spot. He hadn't been spending as much time as he should have with his godchildren. If she'd been trying to give him a guilt trip, those words would have done it, especially given the reason he was here.

"Grab another sheet from the linen closet in the hallway, and grab a few more books from the shelf," she instructed. "Oh, and get a chair from the kitchen. Drape the end of your sheet across the card table and onto the chair. That'll give us all a bit more wiggle room. Believe me, these two are regular squirmy wormies."

By the time he'd followed all her instructions and lengthened the makeshift tent, she was fully absorbed reading the twins their book. He stood before them, wondering how he was going to get where Miranda wanted him to go.

She flashed the cover of the book at Simon, as if finding out what she was reading would somehow convince him to crawl in.

"We're reading *Little Red Riding Hood*. Hudson likes the wolf, don't you, buddy?" she asked the baby, making a growling sound and tickling his tummy.

Hudson squealed and giggled happily.

"Tell Uncle Simon you want him to come on down," she said to Harper, giving her the same affectionate tickling treatment Hudson had just received. "I think he's being a little bit stubborn, don't you?"

Simon balked at her words. He wasn't being stubborn. He was being practical.

And this was definitely *not* how this confrontation was supposed to go. He hadn't envisioned anything of the sort when he'd first knocked on her door, but then, how could he have? This whole scenario was mind-boggling.

He was losing his momentum by the second and he couldn't seem to do anything to stop it.

"But this is—" he started to say.

Ridiculous.

Humiliating.

Mortifying.

She raised a jaunty, dark eyebrow. There was no question about it. She was outright daring him to make a fool of himself with the twinkle in her pretty hazel eyes.

This was nuts. He was crazy just to be thinking about it.

There was no way he was going to get out of

this with his dignity intact. But he'd never been the type of man to walk away from a challenge.

Not now. Not ever.

Grumbling under his breath at the ignominy of it all, he dropped onto his belly to army crawl into the ~~mixed-up files of Miranda's imagination~~ makeshift dwelling.

"Pirates or spaceships?" she queried as he settled himself in. Grinning, she passed him a handful of crayons.

"Uh—spaceships, I guess." Not that he had any real preference for one over the other. He'd honestly never given it any thought.

"So in your most secret heart of hearts, you long to be an astronaut and not a cowboy, right?"

Absolutely not.

He supposed he *had* imagined exchanging his cowboy hat for a space suit when he was a child—but his *childhood* had gone by in the blink of an eye, almost as if it had never really existed at all.

Reality was reality, and he was a cowboy.

Sort of.

"Yeah. I guess I did. When I was a really little tyke. Maybe three years old."

Back before his mother—a single mom herself—had gotten thrown into drug rehab one too many times. Before social services had gotten their hands on him and he'd been tossed into the pitiless foster system and left to sink or swim. His childhood dreams had morphed into a nightmare that he couldn't wake from.

"Coloring is another way of dreaming, you know."

Simon scoffed softly. He knew better. He had dealt with far too much reality in his life for him to imagine anything past the trials of the day. Scribbling on paper wouldn't change a thing.

And dreaming? That was a fool's errand.

He was a responsible man now. He colored black-and-white, inside the lines. But when Harper batted her hand at his coloring book and babbled her baby nonsense at him, he took a blue crayon and started filling in the page before him.

"So, you're not an actual, live spaceman," Miranda said with a mock frown of disappointment. "What do you do for a living, then?"

"I breed and train cattle dogs," he explained as he switched a blue crayon for red.

"I don't know why, but I assumed you'd grow up to be a rancher like Mason."

He shrugged. "I'm not really cut out to be a rancher," he explained. "I can ride a horse and rope a cow, but I didn't grow up in the country. I didn't live on a ranch until I was sent to the McPhersons in Wildhorn when I was a teenager. Training dogs is a better fit for me than herding cattle."

Dogs were reliable. They loved unconditionally. Not like people.

He didn't give his trust easily. Bouncing from one foster family to the next as a kid had taught him to depend on only himself. He wasn't much in the relationship department, either. He'd never really learned how to make a relationship work out. He was broken. Like the Tin Woodman in *The Wizard of Oz*, he was fairly certain he didn't have a heart.

It was hard enough to learn how to rely on God, never mind people.

He paused. "I do own an acreage with a few head of cattle, and I like the hat."

That wasn't exactly a rarity. Nearly all the men in Wildhorn, Texas, wore cowboy hats, from the time they were old enough to sit in a saddle until the day they were laid to rest. Even the local florist sported a Stetson.

"I remember when you moved to town," she admitted, her cheeks coloring under his gaze. "You were in tenth grade. I was in seventh."

He couldn't imagine why she would recall that, other than that he and Mason were such best buddies. He'd never been a popular kid and hadn't had many friends. The truth was, he hadn't made much of a mark in Wildhorn, then or now, and what he had done he wasn't proud of. He had a lot of ground to make up for.

"I never had a dog, even though I grew up on this ranch," she said thoughtfully, referring to the Morgan holdings, on which her cabin rested. "We only kept ranch animals. We had a couple of herding dogs and a mean-spirited barn cat, who never let me anywhere near him. Once I started my photography career, I was traveling too often to consider a pet."

"That's a shame. There are many reasons to have a dog, the least of which is that they are good for your health. And they are the perfect companions. They're easy for anyone to care for."

He probably sounded like a commercial, which he kind of was, since dogs were his life's passion.

She grinned. "Trust me, I'm the exception to that rule. When I was about ten years old, my mom put me in charge of the garden for exactly one season."

Why was she talking about plants?

"Nothing grew but weeds. No vegetables thrived, and hardly any of the flowers bloomed. I took my mother's beautiful, colorful garden and murdered it.

"When I lived in my loft in Los Angeles, I experimented again and tried keeping a cactus. You know—the kind that don't need a lot of attention. Mary helped pick it out. She was the real green thumb of the family. She told me plants helped clean the air."

She stopped and swallowed hard. He didn't need her to tell him what she was struggling with, how fresh her grief must still feel for her. It was written all over her face, and tears glittered in her eyes.

Immediately, his innate masculine protective instinct rose in him, but he didn't trust female tears any more than he did the crying woman so he quashed it back.

Still struggling to speak, Miranda cleared her throat.

"Mary assured me a cactus was the easiest to keep and that even I couldn't fail, but I managed to strangle the life out of the poor thing within a matter of months."

"You forgot to water it?" He managed to keep his voice neutral, but he couldn't help but be concerned. If she was afraid of owning a houseplant or a pet, how was she going to get on with twin *babies*?

"Sometimes. I'd go weeks without thinking about it at all, and then I'd suddenly remember and overwater."

Her face flamed.

"Anyway," she said, taking a deep breath and swiping a palm across her cheeks to remove the lingering moisture, "at the end of the day, I destroyed it. What's the opposite of green thumb? Black thumb? That's me."

He chuckled despite himself.

"So you can see why I'd be concerned about owning a dog. Fortunately, I don't need a live animal to keep me healthy. I'm in good shape. I work out and eat clean, most of the time. Barring chocolate. Chocolate anything is my weakness."

She *wouldn't* be concerned about her physical condition. She was in really good shape—objectively speaking.

"You could use one for good therapy, then. Dogs make great listeners."

He didn't know why he was trying to sell her on the benefits of owning a dog. He wouldn't put one of his dogs in her care in a million years. She had more than enough responsibility with the twins.

She laughed. "I guess we can all use a little good therapy from time to time, can't we? I imagine a dog is far cheaper than a psychologist."

"And a therapist isn't overjoyed to see you when you walk in the door at night like a dog is."

"Point taken." Miranda helped the twins change their crayons to a different color.

He didn't want to like anything about this woman, but he had to admit she did already appear to have somewhat of a handle on keeping the twins occupied and happy. Much better than he'd thought she would have, in any case.

"So tell me about *your* dogs." She propped her chin on her palms.

He raised a brow. Most people's eyes simply glazed over when he tried to talk about his life's passion, yet Miranda was urging him to do so.

"My herding dogs are the way I make my main living," he said. "I own a few especially well-bred Australian cattle dogs with excellent working lines, and between all my females, I manage several litters of puppies every year. I train them and sell them to local ranchers in Texas and surrounding states. I've developed enough of a reputation that I've got a waiting list for my puppies. That's my bread and butter."

He didn't know why he was telling her all this. He hated talking about himself and didn't like to brag. But there was something about Miranda's personality that pulled the words right off his tongue.

Harper rolled over and stared up at him with her big brown eyes. He planted a kiss on her chubby cheek, making her smile and pat his whiskered face with her soft palm.

"I have a dog rescue on the side, and that's where my true life's work lies," he continued. "I take dogs from kill shelters and help them find forever families. That's the name of my shelter—Forever Family. But some of the dogs I pick up have health or behavioral issues and can never be rehomed, so they stay with me."

Her eyes widened. She was probably imagining how many dogs he sheltered. She would be surprised when she knew the truth, because she was probably guessing too few.

"I teach all my dogs—cattle dogs and rescues alike—to pass the American Kennel Club Canine Good Citizen program. That certification goes a long way into making the dogs more adoptable."

"How interesting," she said, and sounded like she meant it. "All the shelters I know just keep the dogs in cages and walk them from time to time. It's commendable for you to put in the extra effort to make them ready for their new adoptive families. And I imagine there aren't too many people who would be willing to take on a dog that they knew at the outset they couldn't rehome."

"No, I don't suppose—" Suddenly, he clamped down on his jaw and lowered his brow. Why was he continuing to yammer on about his work? It made him feel vulnerable that he'd shared a part of himself that he rarely revealed to others.

In general, he kept his thoughts to himself, and this—*this* was Miranda Morgan he was opening up to, telling her all about his life.

His guard snapped up. He sure as shootin' hadn't come to visit her on a social call, much less to put himself in the hot seat—or underneath a makeshift tent with crayons in his hand.

This was ludicrous. How was he going to turn the conversation around to the real reason he was here?

"No, no, Hudson," Miranda said when the boy started gnawing on the end of his crayon. "That's not your snack." She reached into a plastic bag she'd stored beside her and withdrew a hard cracker, replacing the crayon with the finger food.

Simon didn't want to be, but he couldn't help but be impressed.

Again.

The woman had actually considered that Hudson and Harper might want snacks before she'd arranged the twins—and herself—in the tent.

Miranda had been a single socialite and suddenly she was a mother. She couldn't possibly have adapted to her new role as much as it appeared she had. He must be seeing something out of the ordinary, catching her in an especially good moment.

But he had to admit she seemed to have thought of everything. He knew he wouldn't have fared so well, despite having known and interacted with Hudson and Harper since their births. He would have gone in with nothing and would have had to crawl in and out of the tent every time the twins needed something else.

He wouldn't have even thought of the *tent*.

He hated to consider the possibility, but apparently, despite that she'd just arrived in town and had only been the twins' official guardian for a few days, there was something Miranda could teach him about caring for babies.

Who knew?

Miranda handed Simon a cracker and gestured for him to give it to Harper, who'd pulled herself to a sitting position and was manipulating a toy cell phone, pushing buttons that made beeping sounds.

So Miranda had thought of toys, as well.

Simon tried to give Harper the cracker, but unlike her twin brother, she completely ignored his offering.

"What am I doing wrong?" Simon asked, his cheeks burning. He was glad his jaw was covered with a few days' growth of whiskers to hide the fact that he was flustered by his inability to get Harper's attention.

Miranda chuckled. "That's okay. Don't sweat it. You aren't doing anything wrong. Hudson will eat Harper's cracker if she doesn't want it. He'll graze all day if I let him. Snack after snack between meals. I think he's on a growth spurt."

"My godson's getting to be a big, strong boy," Simon said proudly.

"Typical guy, right?" she teased. "Eating everything put in front of him and then some. But don't worry. Harper can hold her own with Hudson," Miranda assured him. "When she wants to."

Typical woman, Simon thought, but did not say aloud.

"In general, Harper's more easily distracted by books and toys than food. It's one of the main differences I've noticed between the two of them. That and the way Harper babbles so much more than Hudson. She likes to look you right in the face and *talk*."

Also typical woman.

Simon filed that information away in the back of his mind. He welcomed anything that would help him get to know the twins better.

"How about you? Would you like a snack, *Uncle Simon*? Since we're camping out, we don't have as much variety as we would if we were hanging out in the kitchen, but I can offer you a cheese stick and a box of juice."

He grinned and shook his head, thinking she was teasing him.

"Your loss." She shrugged and handed Hudson and Harper sippy cups, then pushed a tiny straw into a box of juice and peeled a cheese stick for herself.

He thought she must feel silly chowing down on a toddler snack, but she didn't even appear to notice how incongruent she looked, gnawing on a cheese stick underneath a tent that was too small for her and then taking a long, noisy slurp out of a boxed juice.

"The first day here, I bought the juice boxes for the twins. Turns out they weren't quite ready, so this is my new go-to drink." She saluted him with the juice box.

It was as if she embraced her inner child or some nonsense like that. And yet there was something about her innocent actions that warmed Simon's heart—and then sent it scrambling backward in retreat.

Oddly, she made him feel like an old codger with his shirt buttoned all the way up to the neck, stiff and set in his ways.

He yanked on his collar, even though in reality he wore his chambray with the two top snaps open.

Her smile widened, as if she'd read his mind. "Sometimes I feel more like a kid than an adult."

She appeared to realize how that sounded the moment the words left her mouth. Her expression immediately turned apprehensive and she dropped her eyes so her gaze no longer met his.

"Um—that probably wasn't the best thing to admit, was it? Sometimes my mouth runs faster than my head."

He rolled to his side and couched his head in his hand.

"Probably not," he agreed as he schooled his thoughts to take advantage of this perfect opening. "We need to talk about that, actually."

Her gaze widened. "W-what?" she stammered, clearly taken aback, either by the sudden change in his mood or the way he'd narrowed his eyes on her.

"I'd prefer not to speak to you in front of the children," he said.

The twins might not understand the words, but they would probably pick up on the tension, because he already knew he was going to get flustered and he doubted his ideas would go down well with Miranda.

Her gaze widened. "Oh. I…see."

Clearly, she didn't. But she'd picked up on his change of attitude and her shoulders had tensed.

"It's about time for me to put the babies down for their naps, anyway."

She switched her attention to the twins and her expression lightened.

Harper snatched at the cracker Hudson was busy gnawing on, taking it away from him. Hudson howled in frustration. Miranda laughed and handed him another cracker.

Harper let out an ear-piercing screech, as if someone had pinched her. The guilty party, cracker crumbs on his chubby cheeks, darted forward, right out of the tent. The kid army crawled faster than any soldier Simon had ever seen.

Without thinking, Simon shoved his knees under him and went up on all fours, smacking the back of his head on the card table and sending it keening to the side.

Stretching to his full length, he grasped Hudson by the waist and scooped him into his arms on a roll, landing on his back with Hudson flapping on his stomach.

"Where do you think you're going, little buddy?" he asked, planting an affectionate kiss on the baby's forehead. "Did you pinch your sister? Gentlemen don't pick on ladies, even when they deserve it."

"Simon?" called Miranda, her voice sounding oddly muffled from behind him. "Harper. Ow!"

When he glanced back, it was to find the card table tipped completely on its side. Harper was sitting by Miranda, laughing and batting her arms as she pulled her fingers through Miranda's long chestnut curls.

Miranda couldn't stop the baby from yanking and tugging, even though it had to hurt, because somehow, she'd managed to get completely rolled up, cocoon-style, in a couple of the white sheets that had only moments before served as a tent.

"A little help here?" she pleaded around the

cloth. She wriggled but only managed to wrap herself tighter and tighter.

"Ironic, isn't it?" he asked mildly as he placed Hudson next to Harper and started tugging at the sheets tangled around Miranda.

With effort, he gently unwrapped her.

"What?" Her brow narrowed in confusion when she noticed him staring at her.

He paused significantly.

"You're a *mummy*."

So not funny.

At least, coming from Simon West it wasn't. He'd been a callous teenager, and it didn't look like he was much better now. His mood had gone as dark as a thunderstorm.

After putting the twins down in their cribs for a nap, Miranda dragged her feet as long as possible before returning to the kitchen, where she was oddly certain a confrontation was going to take place. About what, she had no idea.

She'd never been the confrontational type. She preferred to keep the peace.

Simon had been nice enough for a while, but his surprise visit, especially the whole *we need to talk* thing, definitely had the edge of tension around it.

She serenaded the twins with an extra lullaby and lingered by their bedsides until they dropped into a tranquil slumber. She loved the sound of their deep breathing and cute little snores.

Here in the quiet of the nursery it was nice and calm, and Miranda's heart teemed over with serene warmth and love, the polar opposite of the crazy, uneven pulse-pounding her heart had taken with her surprising and unexpected encounter with Simon West.

Simon, the boy Miranda had crushed on for every angst-ridden day of her teen years, was now a man whose once soft adolescent face had been hardened by life but was no less handsome for whatever trials the years had given him.

Along with her brother Mason, Simon had picked on her incessantly when she was a soft-hearted, impressionable teenager, but that hadn't kept her from crushing on him. There was one prank in particular that had stayed with her that had, in a way, informed the woman she'd become when she'd left Wildhorn to pursue a career in photography in Los Angeles.

He probably didn't even remember the hurtful incident that had so mortified her, and if he did, it was probably only as a humorous blip on his radar.

She scoffed softly and shook her head. She'd just been a silly lovesick teenager. It had been a long time since high school, and she'd tucked her memories of Simon, both the nice and the not-so-nice, deep into her heart and locked them away for good.

Or so she'd thought.

Naturally, she'd known when she'd moved back to Wildhorn that Simon would eventually cross her path. He and Mason were still best friends.

But she wasn't in any particular hurry to see him again, and she definitely hadn't expected the explosion of emotion she'd felt when he'd walked in the door of her cabin and she'd first met his sea-blue-eyed gaze. It was as if a boxful of fireworks had suddenly gone off in her chest.

Oh, she remembered Simon, all right. So much more than she wanted to admit. She still recalled every detail of her high school years, every single time she'd lingered by his locker in hopes of seeing him, or stared up at the ceiling in her bedroom, listening to sad songs and pining for the boy in the next room playing video games with her brother.

As an adult, she'd had her heart thoroughly broken by a man using her to further his career. She'd learned from that, and her trust didn't come easily anymore. She'd sealed up her heart and intended to keep it that way.

Which was all the more reason for this first encounter with Simon not to be an emotional explosion.

She'd been so *certain* she'd prepared her heart

for the eventuality of seeing him again, now that she was home. That any silly teenage emotions she'd felt for him were far behind her.

Clearly not so much.

And anyway—why *had* he mysteriously shown up at her cabin, insisting that he wanted to talk to her?

She blew out a breath and straightened her shoulders. It wasn't doing her any good to hide in the nursery speculating over what he might be doing here. The only way she would find out what Simon wanted was to talk to him.

With a sigh, she gave the twins one last loving glance and quietly closed the door to the nursery behind her.

The first thing she did when she entered the kitchen was grab the baby monitor and place it on the table between them like a shield as she slid into a chair across from Simon. She'd brewed coffee earlier in the day, and he'd taken the initiative to pour them each a cup and warm the brew in the microwave.

"Cream or sugar?" Miranda asked, taking a fortifying sip of the hot liquid.

He shook his head. "Dark."

Kind of like the look he was giving her right now.

"I'm going to come right to the point," he said, moving straight past polite niceties and digging right in. "I have some concerns about Mary naming you the twins' guardian when Mason and Charlotte clearly would have been the better choice."

She choked on her coffee.

Of all the rude and unconscionable declarations he could have made…

His words were so blunt they hit her like a sledgehammer. She scrunched her brow and bit the inside of her lip in a desperate attempt to keep him from seeing how much his statement had hurt her.

"And this is your business how?"

He lifted his chin and narrowed his now ice-blue eyes. "I have a vested interest in them and have every intention of protecting them. I expect to have the opportunity to spend time with them and really get to know them. I'm their godfather, which you would have known if you had bothered to attend Harper and Hudson's christening."

"Wow. Judgmental much?"

"Just telling it like it is."

Miranda's first impulse was to argue with him, except for one tiny detail—

He was right.

She *had* missed the twins' christening, something that she now deeply regretted. If she could dial time back…but she couldn't. All she could do at this point was own up to her past mistakes and move forward from here.

"You're right," she admitted softly.

Simon looked as if he was about to speak, but then he cut himself short and stared at her open-mouthed.

"I'm sorry. Did you just say I was *right*?"

Clearly that wasn't the response he'd expected. For a man who didn't know her, he certainly had his opinions about her firmly in place.

She couldn't help but be a little resentful, but she pressed back the prickly feelings in her chest and continued.

"I wasn't at the babies' christening, and I should have been. With John's schedule as a surgeon, Mary and John were only in Wildhorn for that one weekend. They couldn't change their schedule, so I should have. No matter what my reasons, I let my career take precedence over my family, and there's no excuse for that, so I'm not offering any."

Once again, he hesitated before speaking.

"Special client?" he guessed, curling his hands around the mug of coffee.

"A-list actors in a private ceremony." She sighed. "It wasn't about money or prestige. Both actors were and are close personal friends of mine. The wedding had been planned for a year in advance and I had committed to shooting it well before the twins were even conceived, never mind born. In any other circumstances, I would have excused myself from the shoot and found another photographer to take my place for them."

"That probably wouldn't have been a good move for your career, though, right? You wouldn't want to be seen to be reneging on your obligations," he said drily.

She couldn't tell whether he was beginning to see her side of the story or whether he was trying to coax her into digging herself deeper into the muck of remorse and shame. Not that it mattered either way.

"Maybe. I had a reputation for being especially trustworthy. But I would have survived, even if my career took a hit. As it is, now that I'm stepping into my new role as Harper and Hudson's mother, my celebrity photography days are history, anyway. So in the long run, it didn't really matter."

She felt slightly nostalgic at the admission, but surprisingly not sad or regretful. She'd left celebrity photography in the past, where she now knew it permanently belonged. How could it be otherwise?

It didn't matter if she'd made the decision to forage into the realm of motherhood unaided by circumstance, or whether she'd been thrust into the role by a tragedy. She had done everything she'd desired to do in her career, and it was time to come home. Hudson and Harper's guardianship had simply given her a push in the right direction.

Home.

"This must be a jarring change for you, going from the lifestyle you've been leading to living in a guest cabin on your brother's ranch."

Again, she felt as if he was probing for answers beneath the surface and possibly trying to trip her up.

She shook her head. "Don't forget I grew up here. It's not that much of a culture shock for me to return to my roots."

And if it was, she most certainly wasn't going to admit that to Simon. She still had the feeling he was pushing her to justify the decisions she'd now made, just as she had put it all out there about her past and admitted her mistakes.

Well, her decisions were her own, and none of his business.

"You said you want to be a special part of the twins' lives. What, exactly, does that look like?"

She tensed for the answer. She didn't trust him as far as she could throw him, which wouldn't be far, big lug that he was. And she suspected he didn't trust her, either.

"Exactly?" he echoed. "I don't know. You let me in to your life. I let you in to mine. Maybe we can do things once in a while. With the twins, I mean."

He cringed. He literally, actually *cringed*, enough that Miranda could see it in his expression. Was he looking for reassurance that the twins were safe and loved with her? And was it really that distasteful for him to consider spending time with her?

He was certainly no picnic, either.

She narrowed her gaze on him.

"Like what?" she asked warily.

"Take them to the playground. Attend community events together. Maybe have them come meet my puppies. Simple country living."

If that was all it was—and if Simon was really serious about this…

The twins could use another good male role model in their lives. Emphasis on *good*.

If Simon started acting like a jerk, this arrangement stopped.

"I accept."

"Simple country living," he repeated, appearing surprised that she'd relented so easily.

"Yeah. I got that," she said sardonically.

"You won't miss your old life? The parties? The society? The dazzle?"

The truth was, she was tired of the limelight. Even being the one behind the camera, every aspect of her life was exposed to the public eye. A nice, quiet cabin on a remote Texas ranch didn't sound so bad.

Okay, so maybe not *quiet*, what with two babies who made their needs known loud and clear at all hours of the day and night. But private, in any case.

She stared at him for a moment, trying to read his expression, but he did a good job concealing his thoughts.

"I suppose I won't have many opportunities to wear any of the glitzy cocktail dresses I've accumulated, but I can still tote around my designer purses. I'll have the best-dressed diaper bag in town," she joked.

He didn't laugh. He didn't even crack a smile.

He didn't think she was good enough to be Harper and Hudson's guardian.

Well, join the club, buster.

He was going to have to stand in line to claim that particular conclusion, because she'd already tried that one on for size, and unfortunately, it fit.

She sighed wearily. "Look. I get why you're concerned. I don't know why Mary chose me to be the twins' guardian. I only know she did, and I'm going to do the very best I can with what I've been given."

His lips were pressed into a straight line and his expression didn't give anything away. She half expected him to tell her to give up now. That was what he was here for, wasn't it? To bully her?

She might not have as much confidence in her maternal abilities as she would like, but if he was going to press her, she would push right back. She wasn't a vulnerable teenager anymore.

She wouldn't let herself be trod upon by Simon, or by any other man. It had happened once, in Los Angeles. It would never happen again.

Her words were brave, but in the deepest recesses of her heart, the question continued to nag at her.

Could a woman like her really *learn* to be a mother?

Chapter Two

Simon waved as Miranda pulled her tulip-yellow convertible up his long driveway and parked next to his beat-up silver dual-cab truck—a considerably more reliable vehicle in a small ranching town. The tiny two-door looked incongruous next to his old truck and the red barn, which desperately needed a new coat of paint.

It had been a full week since they'd had their confrontation, such as it was. He was still reeling from that one. It hadn't gone anything like he'd imagined it would.

He hadn't expected Miranda to own up to her mistakes, or even to feel any remorse about missing the twins' christening.

But she'd not only felt remorse, she'd shown it, too, throwing Simon off his game. It took a strong soul to do that. At this point he didn't know what to think of her.

The jury was still very much out on Miranda Morgan.

But no matter how he felt about her, now that the twins were living in Wildhorn, he'd have the opportunity to get to know his godchildren better, and he wasn't going to pass up on *that* blessing, no matter what form it had shown up in.

He chuckled as Miranda maneuvered halfway into the backseat in order to release the children from their car seats and pass them out to him. He would never understand why rich folks always bought minuscule sports cars to show off their wealth. No normal-size person could fit comfortably behind the wheel, and Miranda was tall for a woman—and many men.

In all, it took her about five minutes of squirming and stretching to get the deed done. Eventually, Miranda had managed to unfold herself from the backseat and take Harper into her arms.

"I know, I know," she said before Simon could say a word.

He cocked an eyebrow.

"This car is completely inappropriate for the country," Miranda spouted, rolling her eyes. He didn't sense a hint of the annoyance he'd been expecting from her, given that the last time they'd seen each other he'd come at her with a baker's dozen of accusations. "Thank you so much for inviting us to your ranch today to see the puppies being born."

He'd been less than tactful that day at the cabin. He thought she might—or rather, ought to be— upset by their altercation, and his, let's face it, blatant rudeness at times, even if at the end of their conversation they'd come to an uneasy truce. But if anything, Miranda's voice was laced with pure excitement, the same kind of childlike attitude she'd displayed while stretched out underneath her make-believe sheet tent, reading fairy tales with the twins.

"Of course, I grew up on a ranch, so I've seen baby animals born before," Miranda said in the same animated tone. "But never puppies. Birth is such a beautiful thing. The twins will be so excited."

He didn't know about the twins. He suspected they were too young to appreciate the event, although they'd probably enjoy the new puppies.

But Miranda?

Her hazel eyes were sparkling with delight.

He was proud to be able to show off such a vital part of his work, and one of his most satisfying.

He didn't trust Miranda, but he wanted to make sure she trusted him, to see that he worked hard and was successful with his endeavors, that he was stable and dependable, so she would have no questions about him being around for the twins, about him being a good role model for them.

He wanted to *be* dependable and stable for the twins. Be their rock when the world floundered around them. Be the man he'd never had in his life when he was a child.

Of course, by nature his business was anything but stable, but she didn't have to know that.

"I own six female Australian cattle dogs," he explained as he led the happy group into the barn, Hudson in his arms. "All from top working lines. I think I've mentioned a little bit about how this works. I selectively breed them and then train the pups to work cattle using their natural herding instincts."

"I'm impressed." There was an awkward pause, then she smiled.

Her words inflated his ego and he couldn't help but grin back at her. That was exactly what he wanted to hear.

"I get by," he said modestly.

Barely.

Yes, he made a decent profit on the pups, but a lot of work went into preparing them for ranch work, not to mention the vet and feed bills. And it was a feast or famine kind of lifestyle. Funds came in when he sold a litter of puppies, and then he had to make that stretch until the next litter was trained and ready to go to their new owners. So it wasn't exactly like he was swimming in money.

Not like *she* must be. Famous photographer to the stars. Traveling all over the world. Living a lifestyle of glitz and glamour that no doubt made her feel a step above the rest of the world. She probably made more in one day than he made in a good year. There was no way he, a humble cowboy, could even begin to compare to her— not that he wanted to.

"That's Shadow." He introduced the blue heeler to Miranda as she knelt before the cattle dog about to give birth.

"Is it okay if I pet her?" she asked, shifting a now-sleeping Harper onto one shoulder. "I don't want to do the wrong thing."

He studied Shadow for a moment and then nodded.

"Sure. I don't think petting her will be a problem. You'll reassure her that she's got this. I generally tend to stay out of the way when the puppies come and let nature take its course, but I'm always nearby in case she needs help with her delivery."

"She's such a pretty color." Miranda softly stroked between Shadow's ears and murmured gentle, indistinguishable words.

"She's called a blue heeler. I've also got red.

I breed for color, working lines, temperament and health."

Shadow stood up, turned around in her whelping box a couple of times, and then lay down and panted heavily.

"It looks like she's close." Simon crouched down next to the box.

Miranda reached out the arm that wasn't holding Harper. "Here, let me take Hudson so you have your hands free to help Shadow."

Simon didn't immediately hand him over. Unlike the peacefully sleeping Harper, wiggly Hudson was wide-awake and squirming to get down, his thick chestnut-brown hair tufting in every direction, reminding Simon of a rooster. Simon didn't want to set the active baby on the dirty barn floor, even if he'd recently covered the area with a fresh layer of hay.

But holding a sleeping infant and a squirrelly one at the same time would be quite the challenge for Miranda. Hudson was sure to wake Harper up, and she might not be happy about that. Then Miranda would have a vigorous baby and a fussy one.

What did Miranda do during all the times when it was just her and the twins? How on earth did she manage without going stir-crazy?

She hadn't said a word of complaint, at least to him, but she must be exhausted beyond belief. He was only now starting to appreciate her new set of challenges. Even if she was an expert and, as she'd framed it, a natural nurturer, raising twins on her own would be difficult. It was more than he could have handled, were he the one in that position.

He loved the twins, but he didn't envy Miranda. He had to remind himself that she might be putting on a show for him. For all he knew, she was only displaying her good side when the truth was far from what he saw now.

"Hold on a second," he said, keeping Hudson in his arms. "Let me run up to the house and grab a quilt. Then we can put both twins down while we watch Shadow giving birth."

"Good idea," she replied with a grateful smile.

As he jogged up the hill to the ranch house, it occurred to him that maybe he could find some graham crackers or a banana to keep the ever-hungry Hudson occupied. Although a banana might get messy. He'd go with the graham crackers.

Simon found himself grinning and whistling a tune under his breath as he returned to the barn with Hudson in one arm, already munching on a graham cracker, and the rest of the box to share with Harper if she woke, but his joy was short-lived.

As soon as he entered the barn he knew something had changed. Miranda was standing, Harper was crying, and—

His new next-door neighbor, arms akimbo, was hovering over Shadow's whelping box, her expression dire.

This old biddy had caused him nothing but trouble since the moment she'd moved into the active-senior housing development that bordered the land across the south end of his small acreage.

She'd already complained to him about the noise when he'd let the dogs out for a run, both his cattle dogs and his rescues. Cattle dogs needed tons of exercise and the rescues needed fresh air and the chance to stretch their legs.

He usually rode his horse along with the dogs, covering the whole distance of his land, but after Blanche Stanton had lodged her first complaint with him, he'd made a point to drive the dogs in the opposite direction from the housing community.

He couldn't imagine what the old woman was doing here now. She was blatantly trespassing, for one thing. He hadn't invited her to visit his property. What did she think? That she could just nose around in his barn whenever she liked?

Simon's muscles tightened and Hudson made a squeal of protest.

"Sorry, buddy," he murmured before handing the boy off to Miranda and spreading the quilt across the soft bed of hay for the twins, giving him a moment to decide how to approach the unwanted trespasser as he and Miranda situated the babies on the blanket.

"Blanche Stanton," he said drily. "To what do I owe the pleasure of this visit?"

Miranda caught his gaze and her eyes widened. She hadn't missed the dripping sarcasm oozing from his voice.

Blanche obviously wasn't aware that waltzing onto someone else's property was considered trespassing. Or maybe she just didn't care. The hunchbacked, gray-haired old lady turned on him, brandishing her cane like a weapon. It was all he could do not to step back, but he straightened his shoulders and held his ground.

"*More* puppies?" she barked—her voice really did sound like a bark, all dry and coarse. Simon bit back a smile, recognizing that Blanche would be furious if she knew what he was thinking. "You justify bringing more dogs into this world when you already have too many running around this place as it is? This is outrageous. I've a good mind to call the animal control police and report you."

Miranda's brow scrunched over her nose. He could see the wheels of her mind turning as she tried to comprehend the incomprehensible.

"This is what Simon does for a living. He breeds herding dogs."

Miranda sounded genuinely confused, as well she might. In Simon's brief encounters with the old woman, she rarely made a lick of sense.

"What?" Blanche demanded, turning her attention to Miranda. "Who are you?"

"Miranda Morgan. And not that it's any of your business, but Simon raises and trains Australian cattle dogs especially bred for herding," she said, louder and slower, overenunciating each syllable as if somehow that would help Blanche understand what she was saying. "His dogs are supposed to have puppies."

Wow.

Miranda had really been paying attention to what he'd been telling her. His appreciation for her bumped up a notch.

Blanche cackled, but not in amusement.

"Obviously, you don't have the full story, my dear."

Miranda stiffened at the artificial endearment, but her voice was steady when she answered. "Simon has been completely up front with me."

She had no way of knowing that, nor did she have reason to trust him, and yet she was, thankfully, in his corner.

"Ask him what he does with the rest of his time here on the ranch."

"If you mean about his rescue endeavors, he's already told me," Miranda said calmly, tipping up her chin in a silent show of defiance.

Simon was grateful that Miranda was fielding all the questions because he was about to implode, holding back his fury and frustration.

Hudson rolled to the edge of the quilt, gurgling happily and reaching out his chunky arm to grab a handful of hay.

Simon and Miranda reacted at the exact same moment, diving down to rid him of the straw in his little fist before it made it to his mouth. Miranda grabbed the baby and Simon shook Hudson's fist until it was hay-free.

Miranda folded her legs on the quilt and pulled Hudson and Harper into her lap. That was probably a wise move, since Blanche would stand as judge and jury on everything she witnessed.

Simon stretched back to his full height to face his irate neighbor.

"This," Blanche said, her wave encompassing both the dogs and the twins, "is totally unacceptable. It's irresponsible for you to bring babies into this environment."

Simon had to bite his tongue not to snap back at her that this was the country, and that nearly every baby in Wildhorn was growing up on a ranch, many of which had far more animals than Simon, and more variety, at that.

"That's it." Blanche pounded her cane against the ground, but because it was dirt covered with a bed of hay, the tip of the cane didn't make a sound. It was probably not the dramatic impact Blanche had been going for. Simon's eyes met Miranda's and her lips quirked in amusement—at least until Blanche's next words.

"I've made up my mind. I'm calling animal control."

"You do that," Simon said, his voice an octave lower than usual.

He had had about enough of Blanche Stanton. His nerves snapped along his skin and a fire raged in his chest, but the only outward indication of his annoyance was the way his fingers kept twitching into a fist. He couldn't speak to his expression. He forced himself to relax his muscles and shoved his hands into the front pockets of his blue jeans, rocking back on the heels of his boots as if to put more distance between them.

"Now, if there's nothing else," he said through gritted teeth, "you know your way out. And I suggest you take it."

Blanche shook a finger under his nose. It took every ounce of his self-control not to brush her hand away. He stood stock-still, not even allowing air to enter his lungs. He'd probably breathe fire out of his mouth like a dragon if he so much as exhaled.

"This isn't over," she warned.

"I didn't think it was," he snapped back.

He knew as soon as he spoke that he shouldn't have taken the bait. A brief glance at Miranda's wide eyes confirmed that, even if he hadn't created the scene, he was at least an unwilling participant. All he was doing was playing right into the old woman's hands. He knew better than that.

Do not engage.

And yet he had.

It was hard to consider any other way than the way he knew, the defense mechanisms that sometimes rose before he could stop them.

Should he be turning the other cheek here, or was it okay for him to defend his home and his dogs?

Unfortunately, Simon knew all too well that this was only the beginning of his problems with his new neighbor. That Miranda had been there to witness the whole sorry scene only made him feel worse.

How humiliating.

Blanche turned away and stomped a couple of feet toward the door—or at least as much of a stomp as she could make with a limp and a cane—and then slowly turned back to address Miranda, rudely pointing her finger directly at her.

"You'd do well to avoid this one," Blanche

warned, nodding her head toward Simon and sniffing loudly.

He stiffened. The nerve of the woman. Not that he and Miranda had a personal connection, but it wasn't any of Blanche's business if they did. No one had called her in to be judge and jury of his character, especially because she continued to malign him for no good reason.

What if Blanche put doubt in Miranda's mind? Enough to make her reconsider about him spending time with the twins?

He swallowed the gall that rose to his throat at the thought.

Miranda merely lifted an eyebrow. "I'll keep that in mind."

Simon couldn't tell, either by her expression or the inflection in the tone of her voice, whether Miranda was agreeing with Blanche or merely humoring the old woman, but Blanche seemed content with the answer and made her exit.

"Okay, then," Miranda said as soon as Blanche was gone. "Do you want to tell me what that was all about?"

Miranda's naturally empathetic nature—even to a man who tended to be a bully and had issues trusting her—kicked in despite her best efforts to the contrary.

Poor Simon's face had turned a distressing

shade of red, followed by an unhealthy yellowish-green color, as if he was about to be sick.

She could see no reason why the strange old woman had gone off on Simon the way she had.

Over a litter of puppies? What was with that?

Practically all of Wildhorn was working ranch land. Horses. Cows. Pigs. Chickens. Llamas.

Simon's endeavors might veer slightly away from the typical cattle ranch, but he was offering a much-needed product—if you could call a well-bred and well-trained cattle dog a product, or maybe a service—to grateful ranchers in Wildhorn and beyond.

Now that the elderly busybody was gone, Miranda stood and plunked the wriggling twins back onto the quilt in a demonstrative display of rebellion.

Take that, Blanche Stanton.

How *dare* the woman render judgment on her choices where the twins were concerned? The old lady didn't even know the first thing about her. And anyway, it wasn't any of her business if the kids were lying on a quilt in a barn.

Then again, Blanche might be right.

Simon might be right.

Maybe she *wasn't* good mother material. But she was bound and determined to do her very best.

Simon sighed in frustration and picked off

his hat, scrubbing his fingers through his thick blond curls.

"Yeah. I'm sorry you had to witness that."

"Who is she?"

"My next-door neighbor. Or one of them, anyway. There's a small housing development and retirement community along the south border of my land. That woman, Blanche Stanton, moved in a couple of months ago, and she's causing me all sorts of trouble—as you witnessed today."

"Yeah. What is with that?"

"Evidently, she really, *really* doesn't like dogs."

"What kind of person doesn't like dogs?" Miranda asked, realizing even as she spoke the words that, although she didn't exactly *dislike* dogs, it would never have occurred to her to keep one of her own.

"Cat people," Simon joked drily, one side of his mouth kicking up.

"She's probably one of those old ladies who has a hundred cats living in her house. That's why the idea of a dog upsets her so much."

He chuckled. "Maybe."

"I still don't see how it's any business of hers what happens on your property, as long as it doesn't directly affect her. I can't imagine that you allow your dogs to run wild. Or do you secretly let them out on her lawn?"

Simon snorted. "Now there's a thought. But

truthfully, I don't give her any reason to complain about me or my dogs. My property is well fenced, and I almost always ride along to supervise when the dogs go out for their runs."

Simon crouched before Shadow's whelping box and checked her out, then stood and scooped Harper into his arms. It was oddly comforting, watching the big man holding the infant against his broad chest.

"Come on. I want to show you something." He started toward the barn door and then looked back to see if she was following.

She quickly bundled Hudson into her arms. "Should I leave the quilt?"

He glanced at Shadow and nodded. "Yes. We'll be back shortly to attend to the puppies. But there's something I'd like you to see back at my house."

Curiosity swelled within her as she caught up with Simon and walked side by side with him up a small incline to where his ranch house stood. They passed by several dog kennels built underneath a lean-to, but all of them were empty.

When he reached the door, he slid her another glance. "This is, I believe, the real reason Blanche is kicking up such a fuss."

She could already hear what sounded like a dozen barking dogs, everything from a low *woof-woof* to the high-pitched yapping of the smaller dogs.

He opened the door with a flourish. Even though Miranda had some idea what was coming next, she couldn't have guessed at the enthusiasm with which the dogs—more than two dozen in various breeds and sizes—greeted Simon.

He laughed—really *laughed*—as the dogs ran around his feet and nuzzled his hands with their wet noses, begging to be petted.

"These are my rescue dogs." He crouched briefly to accept doggie kisses as he scratched ears and wriggling tail ends.

Was this the same man who, in the past, had such a chip on his shoulder?

The twins gurgled in delight and flapped their arms so hard Miranda could barely keep control of Hudson. Simon tossed Harper into the air amidst much giggling.

Miranda had as many questions as Simon had dogs, but she started with the most obvious one.

"Where is Christmas?"

"I'm sorry?" His eyes widened.

"Thanksgiving was last week and you don't have a single decoration up yet. And no tree!"

"You almost make it sound illegal."

"It should be. Where's your holiday spirit?"

He laughed. "You make up for it at your house."

"That's truly sad," she said, her frown halfway between real and mocking.

He scoffed it off.

"I brought you here to meet my dogs, not critique my lack of Christmas decorations," he chided.

She gave in reluctantly. "You keep all of these guys in your house? I noticed you have some kennels out there, but they're all empty."

Evidently relieved that he didn't have to talk about Christmas any longer, he grinned and bounced up and down to keep a fussy Harper, who wanted to be thrown in the air again, happy.

"Mostly they live with me. They are all crate-trained and I use the kennels we passed by when necessary, but for the rescues that I plan to re-home, living in the house with me helps them prepare for life with their forever families. And the ones who will never be adopted out for whatever reason, well, they *are* in their forever home."

A medium-size, wire-haired dog limped up and bumped Miranda's leg with his snout, and then sat prettily, waiting for her attention. It was only when she reached down to scratch his head that she noticed he was missing one of his front legs.

Miranda felt awkward, not only because she was seldom around dogs, but because this one looked as if it had suffered a major injury at some point. Still, she continued to tentatively scratch the dog's ears and pat his back.

"That's Cumberland," Simon said by way of introduction. "But I just call him Chummy. He was run over by a car on the highway and left to die. But he's a fighter. As you can see, he doesn't let a little thing like missing one leg get him down."

"So you think you will be able to rehome him, then?"

Simon shook his head. "Unfortunately, Chummy has other health issues besides his leg. He'll stay with me for as long as he lives. But to be honest, I've fallen completely in love with Chummy. I wouldn't adopt him out even if I could. He's *my* dog. I have a blind husky named Loki, too."

He whistled and a beautiful husky with gray and white fur trotted directly and obediently to Simon's side. Miranda could hardly tell the dog was blind until she looked into the husky's eyes, which were white and hazy.

"Extraordinary," Miranda murmured, then caught Simon's gaze and held it. "You're not a typical dog rescuer, are you?"

He ran a hand down his face as if he was embarrassed to admit the truth, although Miranda was impressed by the size of his heart. "No. Not really. I don't keep the dogs in kennels until they are hopefully adopted out to new families. I rarely have folks visiting the ranch. Instead, I train them to be AKC Canine Good Citizens and then hold adoption events at Maggie's Pet Store. I've found that trained dogs are easier to rehome, and they make better family members once they're adopted. As for Chummy and Loki—I suppose I just can't say no to an animal in need."

He swallowed hard. "When I first saw Chummy, he was all mangled, and yet his eyes were so hopeful. Even with as much pain as he was in, he let me approach him and take him to the vet. Most people would have put him down, I guess, thinking that was the most humane thing to do. But in my heart I knew Chummy wanted to live. Seeing him all bandaged up with an IV sticking out of him—I almost couldn't stand it. But Chummy recognized me and wagged his tail. He has more courage than I'll ever have."

Miranda's heart warmed. She highly doubted that. In her mind, Simon showed an exemplary amount of courage. She could see how devoted he was to his cause. He was as passionate about his rescue endeavors as she was to her photography, only the work he did helped God's creatures, ministered to those who couldn't help themselves, while hers…had been completely for her own benefit. Publicizing famous people who didn't need any more boost to their egos. The closest thing she got to true charity was photographing high-profile, black-tie charitable events, and even those had mostly been a joke, a way for rich people to feel good about themselves.

"Come sit down for a minute," Simon invited, settling himself on the sofa with Harper on his lap and patting the seat next to him.

Miranda tentatively made her way to the couch, careful to step around the dogs and not on them. She admittedly wasn't the most coordinated woman on the planet at the best of times, and the moving sea of fur made her feel like she was walking on a field of land mines with a baby in her arms.

She breathed a sigh of relief when she finally parked herself safely onto the couch and cuddled Hudson close to her.

"I brought you up here, not only to meet Chummy, but because I have a couple of dogs I'd especially like to introduce to Harper and Hudson," he said.

She flashed him a surprised look. He couldn't possibly think that with all she had going on, she'd want to adopt a *couple* of dogs, or even one.

"I appreciate what you do here," she said, trying to buffer her next words. "But I want to make it clear up front that I have no intention of adopting a dog. They're cute and all, but I've already got my hands full with the twins as it is."

Which was true, but it was more than just a matter of having time to take care of a pet. After seeing the way Simon interacted with his rescues and how excitedly they responded to him, she felt fairly certain she wasn't a dog person.

Other than Chummy, the dogs had mostly ignored her.

"Oh, no," Simon said, raising his free hand palm out. "You misunderstand me. I'm not pulling some sneaky stunt on you to try to get you to adopt a dog. It's just that—well, maybe it would be easier to show you than to try to explain."

"Zig! Zag! Come here, boys."

Immediately after Simon called, two identical small white dogs dashed to Simon's side, their full attention on him.

"Down," Simon said, and both of the dogs instantly obeyed.

Miranda looked from one dog to the other and a lightbulb went off in her head. She understood exactly what Simon was getting at, why she wanted Harper and Hudson to see these particular dogs.

"Twins!" she exclaimed.

Simon laughed.

"Not exactly. They're littermates. Someone dumped them off at the side of the highway, tied in a bag. A Good Samaritan happened to see the bag moving as she drove by and she turned her car around to investigate. Once she realized the bag contained puppies, she contacted the town vet, Aaron Grimes, and he called me."

He helped an overexcited Harper pet one of the dogs, and taking Simon's lead, Miranda helped Hudson scratch the ears of the other.

"Soft fur, see, Harper?" Simon said in the high-pitched tone of voice men tended to use with babies. "This is a doggie."

"Gentle, gentle," Miranda added when Hudson tried to grab a handful of the white dog's fur.

"Zig and Zag are Westies—West Highland white terriers."

"They're very obedient."

He grinned. "We're working on it. Terriers tend to have a mind of their own, kind of like cats. They are one of the harder breeds to train."

Zig licked Hudson's fist and he giggled. Both dogs seemed to like the babies, and the twins were clearly taken with the dogs.

But she'd meant what she'd said earlier. No matter how cute Zig and Zag were, or how much the kids liked them—no dogs allowed. At the moment, suffering cuteness overload, she even had to give herself a stern mental reminder.

She cast her eyes up to make sure Simon understood her very emphatic message, but he was busy helping Harper interact with Zag.

When he finally looked up, their eyes met and locked. A slow smile spread across his lips and appreciation filled his gaze. For a moment, Miranda experienced something she hadn't felt this strongly since, well, since high school—the reel of her stomach in time with a quickened pulse and a shortness of breath.

Either she was having an asthma attack, or else—

She was absolutely *not* going to go there.

Chapter Three

Back in the barn, the strain that had occurred between Simon and Miranda in the house—because he refused to analyze and recognize it as any more than that—appeared to have dissipated as their thoughts returned to Shadow and her puppies. She was still scratching around in her whelping box and the puppies hadn't arrived yet. The twins, worn out from their excitement with the Westies, were both sound asleep on the quilt.

"I usually exercise the dogs by riding around my acreage with them," Simon explained, gesturing to his sorrel quarter horse gelding Dash, who was set up in a nearby stall.

"Some of my rescues like to run more than others. I've got a few couch potatoes who don't want to leave the house, but they all need fresh air and exercise. There's a small lake on the northwest corner of my property that my Labs can't get enough of. They'd stay in the water forever if I let them, and I could toss tennis balls all day and they wouldn't tire of it. I also keep a few head of cattle for the herding dogs to practice on.

"But ever since my first run-in with Blanche, I've been avoiding the land to the south, for the most part. My dogs generally don't go anywhere near the south fences, although from time to time they slip away from me. But I've been more aware of it. No sense stirring up trouble if I can help it. That's why I was so surprised to see her today."

"You don't think she'll really follow through with her threat to call the cops on you, do you? She sounded pretty serious about it."

He shrugged. "She hasn't yet, and she's been making that same threat since the first time she confronted me about my dogs. But it wouldn't surprise me if she did call this time. She was certainly in a tizzy today."

"Yes, but what does she really have to complain about? Everything you do is on the up-and-up, and in my opinion, is a ministry to the animals. There's nothing for an animal control officer to find."

Simon's gaze widened on her and he suddenly had a hard time swallowing around the emotions that had clogged in his throat.

Miranda thought he was doing something special—something she even qualified as worthy of the Lord to bless.

"I do it for the dogs," he insisted, his voice gravelly. It hadn't occurred to him until this moment to give his work to the Lord to bless.

He crouched in front of the whelping box to see how Shadow was faring.

"Exactly," Miranda agreed pleasantly. "For the dogs. That's what makes what you do so wonderful. Plus, I don't know how Blanche can possibly go to the police about this. The woman was trespassing on your proper—"

She cut off her sentence in the middle of a word.

Simon grinned. She must have seen the roly-poly bundle of fur that had arrived when they were otherwise engaged.

"A puppy is here."

Indeed, there was one tiny, squirming puppy being groomed by its attentive mother.

Simon picked up a warm towel from a stack that he had at the ready, heated by a nearby warming lamp.

Gently, he scooped the puppy into his hands.

"Here," he said, handing the pup to Miranda.

"It's white," she exclaimed. "Is that normal?"

"All Australian cattle dogs are born white, but their true colors come on fairly quickly. Back when the breed was first started, Dalmatians were bred into the stock. Hence the white coat."

He put his hands over hers and showed her what to do. Her skin was soft against the calluses of his, and suddenly it felt as if his fingers had thousands of tiny nerve endings crackling.

"Dry him off a bit. Give him a gentle rubdown to help his circulation and breathing. Then we'll put him back in with mom."

"Is he sick?" she asked in dismay.

"What? No," he answered. "This one is healthy, as far as I can tell. We're just giving him a little extra triage."

"This one?" She smiled as her tiny puppy wriggled in her palm. "Does that mean there are more coming?"

"Four more, if the ultrasound was accurate. You can put that little guy back in with his mama now, if you want."

Simon watched as Miranda gently returned the puppy to the warmth of the whelping box. For a woman who'd told him flat out that she wasn't a nurturer, she certainly looked that way to him.

Not just with the puppy, but with the twins, as well, if he was being honest. Maybe he didn't have so much to worry about, after all.

He turned his attention to Shadow, who had just delivered puppy number two, a girl.

He waited until Shadow had cleaned the pup

off and then scooped her into a towel as he'd done with the first puppy and handed her to Miranda. Puppies three and four soon followed, and they repeated the process.

She was staring at him with an odd expression on her face that made his gut tighten.

"What?"

She shook her head. "I'm not— I didn't expect—"

She shook her head and didn't continue.

"One more to go," he encouraged Shadow, running an affectionate hand down her back. "You're doing great, Mama."

Shadow looked spent, but was it any wonder? Birthing was hard work. She flopped on her side where her puppies could reach her belly and lowered her head to the ground, panting heavily.

Simon waited in anticipation. Nothing happened.

Maybe there were only four puppies after all, but Simon's gut instinct, along with his experience, told him that Shadow wasn't finished, even if she wanted to be.

Frowning, he went from a crouch to his knees, pressing his palms against his thighs as he considered what to do.

"That's not good," he murmured under his breath.

"Is something wrong?" Miranda asked, concern lining her tone. She dropped to her knees beside Simon and placed her puppy back in the box, then laid a comforting hand on Simon's shoulder. "What can I do to help?"

Their gazes met and held, hers serious.

"Tell me what to do. We have to be able to do something for Shadow." His stomach twisted when he realized he'd made a terrible mistake asking Miranda to bring the twins and come out to watch the birth of the puppies. At the time, he'd been thinking about the excitement of new life, and he'd been anxious for the opportunity to show Miranda his ranch and the work he did here. But he could have introduced the twins to Zig and Zag at a more appropriate time.

Now, instead of joy, he was handing Miranda a cup full of sorrow, just after she'd lost her sister.

"I'm sorry," he said through a tight throat. "This may not end well."

"Is there anything we can do?" she asked for the third time, her voice calm and containing an inordinate amount of strength.

Shadow stood and turned around in a tight circle. Simon and Miranda looked on intently.

"Possibly," Simon answered softly. "Look—the fifth pup is coming now."

Simon suspected that, like him, Miranda was holding her breath as Shadow strained and panted.

The puppy was large—bigger than his sister.

Usually it was the runt of the litter who ran the risk of not making it through the birth or the first few days, but this puppy was so large Shadow had difficulty bringing him into the world.

Simon didn't wait for Shadow to break the sac and clean up the limp puppy. He had a warm towel at the ready.

"Is he okay?" Miranda's anxious gaze was locked on the puppy.

Simon rubbed the pup's belly, hoping for a welcome wiggle, but the puppy's body sagged.

Lifeless.

Simon kept rubbing, clearing the pup's nose and mouth and attempting to heighten his circulation.

"Come on, boy. You can do it," he murmured.

He cradled the dog's head in his palm and dipped him down and back up again in an attempt to get him to breathe.

Still nothing.

"What can I do?" Miranda asked, her voice surprisingly calm and steady, despite the tears in her eyes. She so desperately wanted to help, and Simon wished there was something she *could* do.

Simon shook his head and continued to rub the puppy, tentatively throwing out a silent prayer. He still felt new and clumsy talking to God.

Please don't let this puppy die.

Losing animals was part and parcel of owning

a ranch, especially because his ranch was unique. He took in rescues that he knew would never recover, and cared for them with all his might, giving them the best quality of life they could have.

And love. These animals needed so much love—as much as they gave.

Dog breeding and rescue was a series of heartache after heartache sometimes, but despite all the pain, the good outweighed the bad, and he couldn't imagine himself doing anything else with his life. There were four healthy puppies to rejoice over.

But Miranda was still freshly grieving her sister. She didn't need to see the hard side of his business.

Not now.

"Come on, boy," he whispered desperately. "Breathe for me."

He performed the same down and up motion but to no avail.

"Give him to me," Miranda said, still amazingly composed as tears silently streamed down her cheeks.

Simon's gaze widened on her but he did as she asked and handed the lifeless puppy over.

Miranda cupped the puppy in one palm and coaxed his jaw open with the other. Then, without hesitating, she put her mouth over the tiny dog's snout and gently blew a breath into his lungs.

She hesitated a moment, rubbing two fingers firmly over the puppy's chest. She blew a breath into his lungs, waited a moment and then blew again.

Nothing happened.

She looked up and her watery gaze met his.

"I'm not giving up," she said as she performed the same dipping motion she'd seen Simon use.

"Miranda." His voice was as dry and coarse as sandpaper as he laid a gentle hand on her arm. He didn't want to lose the pup, either, but—

"I'm not giving up," she repeated firmly.

He nodded.

She blew another breath into the pup's lungs. Then another.

Simon wasn't positive, but he thought he saw— *Yes.*

There it was again.

The puppy squirmed and made a little mewling noise.

"I think that is the most wonderful sound I've ever heard," Miranda said with a relieved sigh.

"Me, too," he whispered in amazement.

Only now did he see that she was shaking. Adrenaline and shock were probably overtaking her.

He took the puppy from her tender grasp and put him in the whelping box for his mother's ministrations, and then turned back to Miranda and took her elbow.

"Sit down before you fall down," he said gently.

She sank gratefully onto the quilt between the twins, both of whom were now awake and wide-eyed.

"Oh," she exclaimed, pulling both children into her lap for an enthusiastic hug, as if reassuring herself that the twins were alive and all right.

"I love you," she said, kissing Hudson's chubby cheek, "and I love you." She kissed Harper's cheek, as well.

"How did you learn to do that?" he asked, still thinking of the magnificent way she'd stepped in and saved the pup.

"What?" she asked, shooting the twins a confused look. "Love the twins? That comes surprisingly natural to me."

He chuckled. "That's fairly self-evident even to the casual observer. I meant what you did with the puppy. Blowing breath into his lungs."

"Oh. That," she said, waving her answer away as if it was nothing special. "As soon as I discovered I was going to be Harper and Hudson's guardian, I took an infant CPR course. I wanted to be prepared for anything."

"Brilliant." Simon wouldn't have thought to do that. Maybe Miranda wasn't as irresponsible as he'd originally thought she was.

"A puppy isn't a baby, of course, but I knew I had to try."

"Well, it worked. And I've never seen anything like it. I think, given that you saved him, that you should name the little guy."

"Really?" Her eyes lit up like firecrackers and her voice once again contained childlike enthusiasm.

He wished he could embrace life the way she seemed to do.

"Okay, then. Let me see." She tapped a finger on her chin. "He's so roly-poly. How about…"

Her gaze met his and her smile coaxed his own mouth into a grin.

"Pudgy."

Chapter Four

Miranda hadn't been to church in ages—other than to photograph the occasional celebrity wedding. She'd been too busy taking pictures and traveling to take time out for Sunday worship—or at least that had been the excuse she used.

And then there had been—she swallowed hard—Mary's funeral. She'd darkened the door of the church for that.

Today she was feeling especially grateful. She was happy for Simon's puppy, which, when he'd called her this morning at her request, he had reported now appeared no worse for the wear. The pup was evidently healthy and robust like his brothers and sisters.

But she was especially grateful for Hudson and Harper and the role she now played in their lives.

Even though they'd changed the vector of her life in a single second, she'd never considered them a burden. If anything, they'd offered her an escape from a life that had become burdensome. She might judge herself and come up wanting as a mother, but that didn't make the twins any less of a blessing.

Today she felt the deep-seated need to return to her spiritual roots, to Wildhorn's small community church, the one she'd been christened in as a baby and had grown up attending every Sunday morning.

When she'd first returned to Wildhorn she'd had no idea what she would find. But reconnecting to her past, to her brother and his family, to her mom and dad, had changed her somehow. Learning the many ins and outs of baby care, and even bumping heads with the handsome, if sometimes irksome, Simon West, she felt as if new life had come into her heart. For the first time in years she felt truly awake, and with that awareness came a reawakening of her heart to God.

She'd just finished bundling the twins in their coats, hats and mittens when Mason knocked on the door of her cabin.

"Ready to go, sis?" he asked, his typical enthusiasm pouring out of him. But she knew he was especially stoked that his little sister wanted to return to the fold.

The evening before, when Miranda had asked if she could accompany them to church, Mason and Charlotte had been overjoyed. Mason told her they'd been praying for her.

She still felt a deep sense of shame that she'd missed Hudson and Harper's christening, but Mason and Charlotte didn't hold it against her. And she knew Mary and John had forgiven her, as well, or else they never would have named Miranda guardian of the twins.

With Harper and Hudson safely strapped in to her sports car, Miranda followed Mason's enormous SUV to church. Even with the largest vehicle on the market, Mason and Charlotte's brood of four barely fit. And Charlotte was pregnant with number five. Talk about loading up a truck to the brim.

Which brought her back to thinking about her own vehicle. She'd loved her little yellow convertible from the moment she'd driven it off the lot. It was a gift to herself, a way to find joy in a life that was often rushed and empty. At least with her car she could control the speed, and she loved the feeling of the wind in her hair.

But a sports car with children?

Not so much.

She'd definitely given her tiny car careful consideration after that humiliating struggle to remove the twins from the backseat as Simon looked on, probably laughing at her under his breath.

She really didn't need flash and speed out here

in Wildhorn. She had nowhere to crank it up unless she sped off down the highway out of town, and there wasn't much call for that right now, what with babies to care for. She was more likely to bend a rim on a deep pothole going up someone's wash-boarded dirt driveway than impress anyone with the zero-to-sixty in ten seconds flat capability of her convertible.

Now that she was Hudson and Harper's mother, she needed a sensible vehicle, one built for country living and something easier to get the twins in and out of.

One more thing of many to add to her ever-growing mental to-do list. She really ought to start writing everything down.

She pulled into the parking space next to Mason and proceeded to unload the twins, trying as hard as she could to maintain her dignity in the process. Thinking of her last foray into unloading them from her vehicle, she'd worn a practical pantsuit rather than a dress, which would have been a total disaster.

Miranda mentally nudged purchasing a new vehicle to the top of her list. She didn't want to lose out on the one opportunity that she had all week to put on a dress.

Miranda's other little nieces and nephews, freshly unloaded from the SUV, pointed at the front lawn of the church and burst into giggles.

She whirled around to see what they found so funny.

Instead of glimpsing whatever sight the gathering crowd was looking at, her gaze was immediately drawn to a broody cowboy on the outskirts of the lawn.

Simon.

He was scowling at whatever had captured the attention of the other onlookers, although she still could not see what, exactly, that was.

The frown that creased his face was almost as deep as the one he'd given her the first time they'd met.

Why was he frowning when everyone else was laughing?

What was eating at him now?

She shifted her gaze, trying to see what was causing such a commotion, but the crowd, snapping pictures with their cell phones and raising a ruckus, was so thick now she couldn't see through it.

She returned her attention to Simon, who was absently curling the brim of his brown Stetson. Miranda thought he might be bending it out of shape. He was so deep in thought, his brow so furrowed that—

"Well, now, that *is* interesting," Charlotte murmured, taking Harper from Miranda's grasp and threading her free arm through Miranda's as if they were two friends in high school and not the mothers of enough children combined to create a basketball team.

"What's interesting?"

Miranda surveyed the area, but she still couldn't see what the gathering crowd was looking at. Maybe Charlotte had caught a glimpse of whatever was so funny and could fill her in on the joke.

"Simon," Charlotte remarked thoughtfully.

"Simon?" Miranda parroted, hoping Charlotte hadn't noticed she'd been staring at him. How embarrassing would that be?

Simon was Mason's best friend, and had been since high school. Miranda didn't want anyone getting the wrong impression about the two of them—especially Charlotte, who knew she'd been spending time with him.

"What about him?" she asked tentatively.

"He's here."

"And this is interesting because—?"

"He hasn't attended church in years, not even on Christmas and Easter. The only time I've ever seen him cross the threshold of a church is at weddings and funerals—and at Hudson and Harper's christening, of course, given that he was named their godfather. Otherwise I doubt he would have been there. Mason said they've been talking a lot about God, but I hadn't realized Simon has come so far in his spiritual life that he is ready to attend church."

Miranda found that kind of odd. For one thing, he didn't look as if he was ready to attend church. He looked like he was about to spontaneously combust.

For another, the first time they'd met after she returned to Wildhorn, he'd made such a big deal about being the twins' godfather, which was a spiritual obligation. Wasn't it?

At the time, she'd just assumed he was a regular churchgoer like Mason and Charlotte were, and that the obligations he referred to in such strong language had to do with his faith.

But if he wasn't here to worship—then what *was* he doing here now?

She'd seen a lighter side of him yesterday, but there was no sign of that man today.

"You and the twins spent some time on his ranch yesterday, didn't you?" Charlotte asked mildly.

"Almost the whole day," she admitted, suddenly reluctant. "He wanted to show us the work he does, and one of his Australian cattle dogs was having puppies."

She wasn't sure she liked where this conversation was going, nor the sudden mischievous sparkle in her sister-in-law's green eyes.

"Interesting," Charlotte repeated.

"Doesn't he look kind of angry to you?" Miranda asked, desperate not to go there. If there was any inkling of past feelings in her expression, a strange by-product of when she'd crushed on Simon as a teenager, she didn't want Charlotte to notice.

Simon was still glaring at whatever was making the rest of the Sunday worshippers laugh in delight and take dozens of pictures.

"Meh," Charlotte said. "Simon is always frowning, unless he's working with his dogs. It's the only time the man's face lights up."

Miranda nodded. She'd witnessed Simon's transformation firsthand. She'd even heard him chuckle a couple of times yesterday.

"That, and maybe the twins. He really cares for them," Miranda added.

"You're right about that. I think maybe you and the twins will be good for him. Won't you, Hudson, sweetheart?" Charlotte tickled the baby's tummy, resulting in a happy squeal and him holding his chubby hands out to Charlotte, who laughingly took him in her arms.

Mason herded his children toward the church entrance and Charlotte followed.

"We'll save you a seat," she tossed over her shoulder.

Miranda nodded.

She hadn't a clue what Charlotte had meant,

nor did she want to speculate. The twins were good for Simon, no doubt about that. But why Charlotte had added her to the picture was a mystery—one that she didn't necessarily want to solve. While it was clear Simon wanted to be included in the twins' lives, she wasn't sure how far he would go to achieve this goal. In her experience, men often acted with ulterior motives—which was why she'd avoided serious relationships altogether, even before the twins had entered her life.

Los Angeles was like living on another planet, completely different from the hometown she'd come from. Everyone looked out for their own best interests in LA, and not so much for the needs of others.

Faith in God was rarely mentioned and practiced even less.

It was all fake. A bad veneer.

The one time she'd opened her heart to a man, it was only to discover he was using her as a stepping stone to further his own career, to make new contacts out of her friends and hopefully get some auditions.

She'd learned her lesson the hard way.

Pastor Corbit stood just outside the red doors of the white chapel, ringing a bell and urging his parishioners inside so the service could start. The crowd dispersed and was heading into the church building, finally allowing Miranda to see what all the commotion had been about.

A life-size, light-up Nativity scene had been set up in the middle of the lawn, a bright, happy reminder of the true meaning of Christmas.

Someone, or maybe a group of someones, had added their own *bright and happy* artistic embellishments to the display.

Miranda put her fist up to cover her mouth as laughter bubbled from her chest. Each figurine in the crèche had been uniquely and colorfully dressed for the season. She was actually impressed with the effort, although she probably shouldn't admit that aloud.

Each of the three camels had different-colored scarves wrapped around their necks. Christmas colors—red, green and gold. The wise men, who no doubt weren't used to the chilly Texas weather during advent season, seeing as they were from the Far East, had been gifted with warm mittens. The usually barefoot shepherds worshipping at the manger now wore sturdy farm boots.

The wooly sheep didn't need much to complete their wardrobes, so they'd been outfitted with sunglasses.

The most humorous member of the ensemble was the donkey, whose long ears had been covered with warm woolen socks.

Inside the crèche, Joseph had been wrapped in a heavy fleece-lined jean jacket, while the Holy Mother was draped in a beautiful royal blue shawl.

The infant Jesus's manger had been neatly covered with aluminum foil that shimmered in the sunshine, and he'd been covered by an old-fashioned homemade quilt.

With her background in photography, Miranda admired the artistry of whoever had pulled the prank. There wasn't anything haphazard about the display. Clearly, a great deal of thought had gone into it.

Pulling out her cell phone, she glanced at the time to make sure she wouldn't be late for the service and then, shifting Harper to her shoulder, began taking pictures from various angles, capturing each of the figurines in a different light. She wished she had her professional camera with her so she could document the scene with the justice it deserved.

As she snapped, she noticed twigs set up as a ranch brand just in front of the Baby's manger.

Three interconnected *H*s—Triple H.

The artists had signed their work, as all good artists did.

Were the pranksters perhaps three teenagers whose first or last names began with the letter *H*?

That was one guess, anyway.

From the corner of her eye she saw Simon staring at her. Or maybe *glaring* would be a more accurate description of his expression.

She stiffened and met his cool gaze with hers, and his disapproving scowl only deepened.

What was the man's problem, anyway?

When she arched her eyebrows at him, he punched his hat back on his head and stalked toward her.

Apparently, she was about to find out what was eating at him.

"Miss breakfast?" she guessed when he stopped before her.

"What?" His frown deepened, if that was even possible.

"You just seem a little…*sour* this morning."

"And I am absolutely *astounded* that you are actually lowering your standards to take *pictures* of this…this…"

"Artistic interpretation of the Nativity?" she suggested.

"I was going to say sacrilegious nonsense." He scoffed and shook his head.

"Frankly, I'm surprised this bothers you so much."

"Yeah? And why is that?"

"Charlotte said you aren't much of a churchgoer."

He caught his breath and jerked back in surprise. "I'm not."

"Then why does this," she asked, gesturing toward the Nativity scene, "matter to you at all?"

"Apparently, you *do* go to church, so I'm going to throw that question right back at you. Why *doesn't* this offend you?"

She didn't bother to correct his false impression of how often she attended church services.

"Because I don't see any malice in it. It looks to me like it's the work of teenagers on a lark."

"Exactly," he said as if she'd just proven his point—whatever that was.

"Look. Whoever it was, they clearly put a lot of planning into it and coordinated it well. No harm done."

"This time," Simon muttered.

Miranda didn't even know what that meant. And she still didn't know what had brought on Simon's bitter mood. But she didn't want him to ruin her morning.

This was her first Sunday back at church, and she'd actually been earnestly anticipating it. Better to change the subject before Simon's attitude started rubbing off on her and she decided to scrap the whole idea.

As far as the Nativity scene went, Pastor Corbit could remove the coats and hats if he found them offensive. It wasn't as if any permanent damage had been done.

"Mason and Charlotte are happy to see you made it to church this morning," she said, hoping her statement would be taken as the peace offering she meant it to be.

She didn't add her own name to that list.

There had been the briefest of moments right there in the beginning, when she'd first spotted him standing by the side of the lawn, that her heart had sparked of its own accord, but that was before she'd seen that perpetual frown lining his face.

Always judging, that one, and as far as she was concerned, he was actively looking to find fault, even when there was none. Miranda. Blanche— although Miranda could sort of see his point there. But he didn't appear to have the capacity to see the good in people.

Only animals. And Mason, but that was kind of the same thing.

Such a shame, but not her problem.

Simon scoffed. "Well, I'm sorry to disappoint Mason and Charlotte, but I'm not here to attend church."

She raised her eyebrows. She didn't have to voice the obvious question—if he wasn't here for the service, then why *was* he here?

He reached into the chest pocket of his burgundy chambray shirt and pulled out a sealed white envelope.

"For the twins," he said, pressing it into her palm.

Before she could open the envelope and see what was inside, Simon had turned away from her and was striding back to his truck.

Miranda stared after him, dumbfounded.

He showed up at church, but not to attend the service?

What was with the man, anyway?

As much as she would have loved to have had time to ponder the answer to that question, or at least open the envelope he had given her, she could already hear the congregation singing the opening hymn.

Great.

Now Simon had made her late for church.

Chapter Five

Simon really *had* shown up at the church this morning with the intention of attending the service for the first time in…well, it had been a long time.

Too long.

But he couldn't very well go in now. Not with Miranda asking so many nosy questions, and then him blurting out that he wasn't going inside.

With a growl of frustration, he loaded himself back into the cab of his pickup and turned for home.

He had a feeling that Miranda was going to continue to be a major pain in his side—and worse yet, she was getting into his head. She could be so sweet, like with the puppy she'd saved, but then there were days like today when they were like oil and water. He never seemed to say the right thing when he was around her. His mind got all muddled up. It was all he could do to keep his boots clear of his mouth.

Women in general were a dangerous species where Simon was concerned. He'd had very few relationships over the years and they'd never gone well. He wasn't great at expressing his feelings, and the ladies he'd dated needed far more from him than he was willing to give—or even *could* give, if the truth be known.

Mason had teased him about becoming a hermit, and maybe he was right. Or possibly an ostrich, burying his head in the sand.

At least his life had been peaceful, before Miranda had arrived with the force of a whirlwind.

He didn't even know how to begin to classify her.

Like how she not only made tents out of blankets, but crawled right in with the children and read fairy tales with separate voices for each of the characters, too.

The way she giggled when the twins giggled.

And why on earth she could possibly think the utter desecration of the Nativity scene had been the harmless work of teenagers on a lark.

No.

More than that.

She thought it was...

Artistic.

He scoffed aloud, even though there was no one in the cab of the truck to hear his disdain.

While he admitted the possibility of it being teenagers joshing around all in fun, as Miranda had suggested, that whole scene was anything but innocent.

Oh, it might start that way, harmlessly goofing around, but Simon had seen it before—how quickly harmless pranks escalated into greater and greater dares and hazing, which eventually became reckless, even dangerous.

He was probably overthinking it, but he'd seen the really bad stuff. Gang initiations. Fighting. Guns.

All of which might very well have started out as an innocent lark.

Another thing that bothered him was that the miscreants who'd gussied up the Nativity scene had felt compelled to sign their work with their mark—a Triple H, whatever that stood for.

Teenagers on an innocent lark didn't tag their work.

Simon had been in enough brawls over the years to immediately expect the worst. He'd been a scrappy kid who'd been on the receiving end of "teenagers on a lark," which had, on more than one occasion, landed him in a Dumpster. He'd started pumping iron in high school and had grown into his height, and all that helped him do was get into more trouble. His reaction today was a defense mechanism, one that had served him well over the years.

Miranda had been born and raised in a good Christian family. Her mother and father remained happily married to this day. Simon supposed he couldn't really fault her for believing the best when she'd never seen anything except happiness in her life.

If he was only thinking of Miranda, he'd probably just let her go on living in her fantasy world, free of all unkindness and crime.

But it wasn't just Miranda.

It was the twins, and Simon had a responsibility to them. He was bound and determined to protect them from anything and everything that could cause them harm, making sure they remained innocent children for as long as possible before they had to deal with the realities of the adult world.

They would have a sweet, innocent childhood, as Miranda had. And when the time came for them to step out into the world as adults, he'd make sure they were street savvy as well as book smart.

Harper and Hudson's uncle Simon would always be there to watch over them, even when they weren't aware he was there.

His heart filled with warmth at the thought of

those two sweet babies. He was truly blessed to be their godfather.

As he pulled up his long driveway, his mind was so focused on thoughts of Miranda and the twins that he didn't immediately see that there was a white SUV parked in front of his ranch house.

An SUV—with writing on the side and flashing red and blue lights across the top.

"What were you and Simon talking about before church?" Charlotte asked as they shared coffee and donuts in the fellowship hall after the service had ended. "It looked pretty intense there for a while."

"*He's* pretty intense," Miranda replied. "It's like he has a swarm of bees inside him just ready to burst out. Or is it just me he's that way with?"

"No, Simon is serious with everyone, all the time—except maybe when he's working with his dogs. He had a rough life growing up. When his mother was forced into drug rehab for the fourth time in as many years, poor little four-year-old Simon was picked up by social services and tossed into foster care, until he was picked up by the McPhersons here in Wildhorn when he was in high school. They gave him the only stability he's ever had."

"I didn't know," Miranda repeated, her heart squeezing in empathy.

"No. You wouldn't, would you? It's not like he's going to come right out and tell you about a past I believe he'd rather forget. He doesn't talk about his childhood," Charlotte continued. "The only reason I know anything is because he's spoken to Mason about it, and he only knows a little bit."

Miranda wondered if she should be hearing all this, if Simon was so private about his past, but it wasn't exactly gossip. Simon had made it crystal clear that he was going to be a big part of the twins' lives. Anything she could do to make her relationship with him easier had to be considered useful information.

"He's a complicated man," Miranda said on a sigh.

"With good reason."

"With good reason," Miranda agreed.

"What's in the envelope he gave you?"

Miranda had temporarily forgotten about the envelope. She was in big trouble if being in Simon's presence, or even merely thinking about him, sent her into a tailspin. She needed to be able to keep her head on straight.

"I don't know. Hold on."

She slid her finger under the seal and withdrew a single sheet of tri-folded printer paper. When she unfolded the blank page, a personal check fluttered slowly to the floor.

Bemused, Miranda picked the check up from where it had landed by her feet.

No explanation.

Nothing.

Just a check made out to her, signed with Simon's scrawled signature.

"What do you make of this?" Miranda asked, setting the check on the table and sliding it toward Charlotte. "He said it was for the twins."

"To help with their upkeep, I imagine. Although—whoa. Two thousand bucks. That's a pretty heavy chunk of change for Simon."

"Really? When I visited his ranch, I was under the impression that his herding dog business was doing very well."

"He's a proud man, but dog training isn't exactly Wall Street. He only gets paid when he sells the litters, so there's a lot of ups and downs, I think. He loves what he does more than making money," Charlotte informed her. "And as you can imagine, every spare cent goes into his rescue.

"There's always something that needs fixing, or they are low on feed, and he's always on credit for his vet bills. Donations cover some of it, but Simon puts in a lot of his personal money, as well."

"Then why would he give me this? I don't understand."

"Because he is the twins' godfather and he loves them. He's always felt a special responsibility toward them, and even more so now that Mary and John are gone."

"And he's worried because I'm their new guardian." It wasn't a question. "Simon doesn't trust me."

"He just wants to do his part, feel like he's contributing to Harper and Hudson's upbringing. I think giving you a check is a discernable, objective way for him to do that."

"There are plenty of other ways for him to be there for the twins besides giving me money, Charlotte. I have more cash in my bank account than I could spend in a lifetime here in Wildhorn. I've already started investment accounts for each of the twins for their college expenses."

Charlotte shrugged, but warning lights sparked from her eyes.

"You'll have to take that up with Simon. But don't be surprised if he throws it back in your face."

"I'd like to see him try. Surely he'll listen to reason. I'm giving it back to him as soon as I see him again."

"Give it your best shot" was all Charlotte could offer.

Simon might be a stubborn cowboy, but Miranda wasn't a slouch in that department, either, and she could hold her own.

She wouldn't have gotten very far in her ultra-competitive photography business if she'd taken no for an answer every time a door started to close in her face. It was because she'd learned how to coax noes into yeses that she'd been able to rise to the top of her field.

One tenacious cowboy wasn't going to get the best of her. If she had to, she would shred the check right in front of him, though she hoped it wouldn't come to anything like that. She had no intention of treading on his ego if she could avoid it.

But she had to make her point crystal clear—she didn't need his money.

If he wanted to help with the twins, surely they could work out some other way for him to be of assistance.

Like teaching them all about the dogs he trained, perhaps, or how to catch a football. Miranda couldn't toss a ball to save her life.

There were a lot of gaps for Simon to fill in, things Miranda had no interest in or didn't possess the required skill set for.

Sports—*all* sports—topped that list.

If Simon was even remotely more coordinated than she was, there was a lot he could teach the twins.

Like many girls, Miranda had dreamed of being a prima ballerina when she grew up, but she'd never made it beyond tiptoeing around the stage with a teddy bear and a tutu before she realized *that* wasn't going to happen.

Then, in second grade, she'd signed up for after-school gymnastics at her elementary school. The program was free and any child could participate—but that didn't, apparently, mean that every child *should*.

After a week of awkward cartwheels and multiple failed attempts at simply leaping over a two-foot-high vault, her physical education teacher had pulled her parents aside and—*strongly*—suggested that she not return the next week. He'd been afraid she was going to seriously hurt herself—and he was probably right about that.

Her teacher hadn't even had to mention how uncoordinated Miranda was. That was a given.

She had cried her eyes out when her parents had told her she wouldn't be returning to the gymnastics class. She'd been so embarrassed at the thought of being rejected. Even a second grader knew when she didn't measure up.

But then, in an attempt to redirect Miranda's thoughts and feelings, Daddy had placed a shiny new camera into her hands. Taking pictures helped her feel better about herself, and she'd discovered something she *did* do well.

At first, she'd photographed landscapes, but she'd soon discovered she was much more interested in turning her lens on people. Faces were ever changing, and capturing unique expressions was both a challenge and a pleasure.

She still couldn't Texas two-step without stomping on her partner's toes, but she *could* take pictures of the party that would last long after the music had stopped and the last decoration taken down.

She had a gift.

And because she'd been able to take advantage of that blessing, she had more money than she knew what to do with.

Miranda retrieved the check from Charlotte, neatly folded it back up in the blank printer paper and returned it to the envelope.

"If I follow you home, do you think you could watch the twins for me for a bit? I don't want to wait to do this. I need to talk to Simon about his check and I'm afraid it might get a little—er—messy. I wouldn't want to subject the twins to that. No need to see their new mama and Uncle Simon arguing over money."

"Maybe it won't come to that."

Miranda hoped not, but she didn't really believe confronting Simon would be as easy as all that. He was a proud man, and after his reaction today, she suspected he might want to take a bite out of her, chew her up and spit her out.

Chapter Six

With his hands fisted and jammed into the front pockets of his blue jeans, Simon reluctantly followed the animal control officer around as he toured Simon's facility.

Officer Kyle Peterson was scribbling in indecipherable chicken scratch on an oversize clipboard. Simon couldn't see what he was writing, but he could guess that the officer was making notes every time he encountered something that, in Kyle's opinion, needed to be addressed or changed.

Was he going to try to shut down the rescue?

And what about Simon's herding dog business?

Simon's lungs felt like sandpaper as he rasped breath after breath.

The animal control officer, whom Simon figured had been alerted by Blanche Stanton, was mostly keeping his comments and judgments to himself, occasionally muttering under his breath as he made his notations. The few times he did stop, point and make suggestions, Simon had to grit his teeth until his head ached.

He suspected Officer Peterson was one of those guys who thought his uniform gave him the right to make personal decrees about a man's life's work, and it wouldn't do Simon any good to argue with him. He was biting the inside of his lip so hard he tasted copper. He'd had run-ins with the law when he was younger and had even spent some time in juvie, and though he considered himself a changed man with great respect for peace officers, this one was giving him hives.

After touring the barn, the officer had made his first few comments and suggestions, ones that had gone completely against Simon's dog handling methods. Simon had briefly attempted to explain his practices and policies, but he soon realized the officer wasn't the least interested in what he had to say.

After what seemed like ages of trailing behind Officer Peterson, the cop finally turned his full attention on Simon.

"Is there somewhere we can sit and discuss my findings?"

The man didn't give away one iota of his thoughts, neither in his gaze nor in his expression. Simon had no idea how bad this was going to be, only that, given the profusion of notes, this could take a while.

"Of course. Come on inside and I'll fix us both a cup of coffee."

Simon realized the gravity of his error the moment the words were out of his mouth. The officer had toured the barn and the grounds, but he didn't yet know what was behind Door #1, otherwise known as the ranch's front door.

"That will do just fine," Officer Peterson said.

Simon picked off his hat and shoved his fingers through his hair as he scrambled for a plan B.

How could he be so stupid?

Puffs of dust swirled through the air from far down his driveway, alerting Simon that yet another visitor was on their way—just exactly what he didn't need right now.

And when he caught sight of that garish yellow sports car bumping along the road, he groaned aloud.

He'd thought nothing could make this moment worse, but he'd been wrong. The *last* thing he wanted was for Miranda to witness this humiliating display.

Yet there she was, plain as day, unfolding her tall frame from the tiny vehicle and heading right toward him. Evidently, she'd left the twins behind, which Simon immediately interpreted as a bad thing.

The twins were the automatic buffer between their dissenting personalities, the oil and water that would not mix.

The officer dropped his clipboard to his side and was giving Miranda an appreciative once-over, which brought out a fiercely protective instinct in Simon that surprised him.

He and Miranda were always bumping heads, except maybe when they were distracted helping the puppies being brought into the world. Why should he care if another man found her attractive?

Because she was the twins' *mother*. That was why.

How dare the man?

"Officer—?" Miranda squinted at the officer's name tag. "Peterson. To what do we owe the pleasure of this visit?"

Simon was instantly aware of two facts.

First was the crafty way she flashed the peace officer a thousand-watt smile that Simon imagined worked on most if not all the men she used it on.

Quite the dangerous weapon.

But not to Simon. Her smile didn't affect him.

Or if he did feel anything, he was strong enough and wise enough to shove it into the back of his mind and ignore it.

The other fact, one which was less obvious but

much more telling—she had referred to them, Simon and Miranda, as *we*. And she had purposefully, he thought, given the officer the impression that she was on Simon's side.

Given the fact that she'd drawn up before a police vehicle with its lights flashing, that was some choice she'd made.

She trusted him.

Officer Peterson. She'd said it so sweetly it immediately won him over.

Why hadn't *he* thought to use the man's name? Make it personal and hopefully a little friendlier. It wasn't like he didn't know Kyle's name.

Miranda had swept right up with her people-pleasing, outgoing personality and had taken everything all in hand within moments, changing the entire tenor of the situation.

Officer Peterson was still gawking at Miranda. If he'd been a cartoon character his eyeballs would have popped out of his head attached to springs and his tongue would have been lolling, but Miranda didn't seem to notice.

"Officer Peterson here just showed up for a surprise inspection on Forever Family," he explained, trying not to sound bothered by the fact. "I'm not sure what it was that precipitated the event."

He was fishing, but the officer wasn't even paying attention to him.

"Oh, I see," purred Miranda. For someone who wasn't a pet person, she sure sounded an awful lot like a cat. "It's such a lovely place, isn't it, Officer Peterson?"

"I—well—" Officer Peterson stammered, his gaze dropping guiltily to his clipboard. He cleared his throat. "You can call me Kyle."

Simon repeated the officer's statement in his mind in a cartoonish voice.

You can call me Kyle.

"Kyle here has just toured our facility. All of the outbuildings, that is."

Simon didn't know why he said *our*. Maybe he was unconsciously referring to the nonprofit organization under which he worked.

Forever Family.

Us.

Yeah, he'd go with that.

"Simon just invited me in for coffee so I can go over my report with him," Kyle said, pulling himself up to his full height, which still left him gazing up at the taller Miranda like a love-struck puppy. "I'm sure Simon wouldn't mind pouring a third cup."

"Inside the house?" Miranda's surprised gaze met Simon's and she raised her eyebrows.

Was he crazy?

She didn't have to say it out loud. He was thinking the very same thing. What did he think he was doing, thrusting the officer into the mayhem of madness that was the inside of his ranch house?

Since Kyle's back was turned to him, he shook his head to let Miranda know he'd realized the consequences too late, and then he pointed a finger at his temple and mock shot himself.

Miranda rolled her eyes.

"You know," she said, linking her arm through Kyle's and giving him her full attention, "I have a much better idea. Simon has a beautiful little lake on his land just over the hill there to the north, and if I'm not mistaken, there's a picnic table with a nice view of the land. Isn't that right, Simon?"

Simon nodded in agreement as he realized where she was taking this. He let out the breath he hadn't even realized he'd been holding. He didn't know why Miranda was here, but he was sure thankful she was.

She pointed to the cluster of trees peeking up just over the rise. "It's too nice of a day for us to be cooped up inside. Why don't you and Simon mosey on down to the lake. I'll bring along a carafe of coffee and see if I can round up a treat of some kind and I'll meet you fellas down there in a minute."

There were so many things wrong with this scenario that Simon could barely start to count them.

Miranda had just enlisted herself in a solo

mission to take on his very messy bachelor pad house, and worse yet, snoop around in his kitchen in order to find everything she needed to serve coffee and treats. He had far more dog biscuits than anything edible for a human, but he thought he still had some packaged chocolate chip cookies left in the pantry somewhere, which he hoped she would find.

He had no doubt that Miranda, maker of blanket tents and encourager of babies' imaginations, could rustle up something for them.

He wasn't worried about the dogs accepting Miranda, but he wasn't so certain about how Miranda would respond to his pack of mutts on her own. They became easily overexcited when visitors arrived, and that was with him there to keep them in line.

At least her gaze had promised him she wouldn't leave him alone with Officer Peterson for any longer than necessary.

Still—a woman poking her nose around his things?

The very thought sent a shiver down his spine.

But then again, she'd successfully redirected the officer away from what would have most certainly been an unmitigated disaster. How would the officer have taken a pack of dogs living in his house? That wouldn't be easy to explain.

Miranda was here.

The thought gave him courage. Unlike Simon, Miranda was gregarious and friendly. She clearly knew what to do and say to defuse even the most delicate of situations.

Well, except for when it was just the two of them alone together.

They sparked like flint on stone.

Regardless, when push came to shove, Miranda had stepped into the ring with him, and he was glad she was on his side, even if that meant she was charming Officer Peterson—Simon refused to call him Kyle—into ignoring, or at least modifying, the many notations on his clipboard.

Simon didn't have the foggiest notion why Miranda was here, sans children—especially since earlier in the day they'd been quarreling over their differing opinions on the defilement of the Nativity scene.

But as he watched her heading toward the ranch house, and hoping Officer Peterson wasn't likewise enjoying the view, Simon decided it didn't matter why she was here.

Only that she *was* here.

And she'd just saved his bacon.

A million conflicting thoughts had rushed through Miranda's mind when she'd drawn up in front of Simon's ranch house and parked her convertible behind a police SUV with the lights still flashing.

Evidently nosy Blanche Stanton had finally made good on her threat to report Simon to the authorities.

Unbelievable.

She and Simon might frequently lock horns, like earlier at church, but that didn't stop her from worrying about him, picturing him being driven off in handcuffs for who-knows-what reason. Her breathing increased into short gasps until she was nearly hyperventilating.

She'd seen him at his worst—with her, obviously—but she'd also seen him at his best, delivering his beloved puppies. She hadn't been around Simon for that long, but it was enough for her to know that he was a man who took honor and loyalty seriously.

She quickly realized he'd backed himself into a corner he couldn't get out of, at least not without her help.

Inviting Officer Peterson into his chaotic, topsy-turvy dog-filled house?

What had he been thinking?

Had he panicked?

Was he insane?

More to the point...

Was *she*?

She'd taken one look at the anxiety in Simon's

gaze, like a beacon warning against sharp rocks just under the water's surface, and her empathy had immediately risen in response. It was a blessing and a curse.

She hadn't actually thought all the way through her brilliant solution to Simon's problem, but she had managed to divert Officer Peterson away from the house with the first idea that had popped into her mind.

Which would have been fine, except…

Now that Simon and Kyle were heading out to the picnic table by the lake, Miranda had a moment to reflect on what she realized was *not* one of her brighter ideas.

Yes, she had distracted the officer from entering Simon's dwelling, but now she'd effectively volunteered herself in his place.

Brilliant move, that.

An animal control officer at least presumably knew all about dogs and would know how to handle himself around them.

Miranda, on the other hand, knew exactly nothing.

She understood why Simon didn't want the officer to know he usually kept all of his rescues in his house, not to mention all the throw-away dogs who made their permanent home with Simon.

Even though Miranda knew next to nothing

about rescue work, she was fairly certain Simon was the exception to the rule. All the dog rescues she'd ever seen—albeit only on television and not in real life—had dogs in kennels, sad eyed and lifting their heads to join the cacophony of barking. Foster families might get involved in individual cases, possibly, but she imagined there was no other rescue that worked remotely close to the way Simon ran his operation, with his entire pack of mutts making their home in *his* home.

That might be difficult to explain.

Which brought her to her second concern—she'd only been in Simon's house once, and she wasn't sure what his dogs had thought of her even then. She wasn't exactly a dog person, and she was pretty sure the canines knew it.

What if she walked in and they thought she was an intruder?

She stood at the entrance to his home, blowing out a breath and shaking out her tense muscles.

She was certain she'd read somewhere that animals could smell fear, and that trait was rolling off her in waves.

What if the dogs trounced on her?

But Simon had immediately agreed to her suggestion when she'd made it, so he must not have been too worried—or else he was so distracted, or so desperate that the officer not see the inside of his house, that he was willing to sacrifice Miranda.

"This is the stupidest idea I've ever had," she muttered aloud as she turned the doorknob. "Well, here goes nothing."

She took two steps into the house and froze as dozens of doggie eyes peered up at her expectantly.

For the first few seconds not one of them moved or made a sound, and neither did Miranda.

Ignore the dogs, get the coffee and get out.

She felt like she was participating in some kind of covert op for a spy agency, except that she'd already been made by every doggie in the room.

Then the chaos started—low woofs, high yaps, and dogs of all shapes and sizes bound and determined to get her attention by every means they had.

Wet noses bumped her palms and tiny paws scratched at her ankles. Oddly, though, even with the frenzy of movement and the cacophony of howls, yips and barks, Miranda realized she was not afraid.

These were Simon's dogs.

He'd taken them in. Trained them. Loved them.

And he trusted them enough to send Miranda into his house unaided.

Three-legged Chummy, the wire-haired terrier,

and Loki, the blind husky, greeted her and she reached down to scratch the dogs' ears.

"All right, fellows—and ladies," she amended. "Let's find the coffee."

Chapter Seven

Simon's neck and shoulders rippled with tension.

What was taking Miranda so long?

It had seemed like hours since he and Officer Peterson had reached the lake and silently seated themselves on opposite sides of the picnic table. Simon had given Kyle the side with the lake view, not so much as a courtesy as that Simon would be able to see Miranda approaching.

He had no way of knowing how long they waited. He didn't wear a watch and he couldn't very well pull out his cell phone to check the time with a cop sitting on the other side of the table. It was probably minutes, but the ticking of seconds in Simon's head grew louder and louder with each passing one.

He had thought the officer would get down to business straightaway—delineating the notes on his clipboard for Simon, rather than waiting on Miranda.

Simon wished he would. It would be far less humiliating for him to face the confrontation alone, because he was well aware that Officer Peterson was about to give him a good dressing down.

Why else would he have made so many notes on his clipboard?

Yet Kyle, as he'd invited Miranda to call him, appeared to be lingering, waiting for her to return.

At long last Simon spotted Miranda jogging down the hill, a coffee carafe in one hand and three cups in the other, as well as a canvas bag Simon guessed carried chocolate chip cookies.

"Sorry for the delay," she said, her breath coming in gasps as if she'd run a marathon and not the short distance from the ranch house. Her cheeks were flushed a pretty pink and the smile on her face was contagious.

Simon's lips were curving upward well before he remembered Officer Peterson was still there. And a quick glance at that man confirmed that he, too, was taken in by Miranda's vibrant expression. The officer was grinning from ear to ear like a mule eating briars.

Simon lowered his brow. Officer Peterson had

better stick to his official business and not go off flirting with Miranda.

After all, she was now the new mother of twins. She didn't have time in her life for frivolity and dating.

Simon had no idea how he would stop such a situation if it occurred, and if she knew he was putting himself up as her personal protector, she'd probably have more than a few sharp words to say to him.

Like that it was her life and he should keep his nose out of it.

But it wasn't just her life. It was the twins he was thinking of.

Mostly.

So he was going to keep his proverbial mantle of protection around all three of them—without ever saying a word to let on.

He wasn't foolish enough to risk his own neck.

Miranda passed out the coffee mugs and laid out the contents of the canvas bag—sugar and creamer for the coffee—for the officer, he assumed, as he knew he and Miranda both drank their coffee black. She'd found the chocolate chip cookies Simon had been fairly certain were in the pantry, and she'd included an assortment of fresh fruit.

"Now," she said as Simon poured each of them

a cup of coffee, "what seems to be the problem here, Officer?"

To his credit, Officer Peterson's expression turned serious. Simon breathed a moment's relief before he remembered that *that* wasn't such a good thing, either.

"Let's start with your fences," Kyle said, addressing Simon, though his gaze occasionally strayed to Miranda.

"What's wrong with my fences?" He knew he sounded defensive, but really. He was meticulous about keeping his fences in order—metal posts reinforced by chicken wire, safe for the sake of the dogs as well as the cattle.

"I'd like to address the southern border in particular. The new retirement community's home owner's association requires eight-foot privacy fences between properties. Building your own will assure you of *your* privacy."

"I don't see how any of this has to do with me. My land isn't part of any HOA. There are already privacy fences on the houses. Why do I need to build one on my land?"

"You are right about the fences already around the houses, and you're also correct that you aren't under any obligations here. But I think it would be in your best interest to consider building one anyway. There's a perception—" he started, then stalled. "One of your neighbors—"

"Has been complaining," Miranda finished for him. "We already know that. But is a new fence really going to solve the problem? I believe the woman is a—how can I say this delicately?"

She grinned and tapped her finger against her lips as if carefully considering her words, although the glimmer in her eyes told Simon she already knew exactly what she was going to say.

"Busybody. Yes, that's the word I was searching for. She's complaining just to hear herself talk. I'm not sure a fence will help with that."

Kyle cleared his throat. "I'm not supposed to say anything, but—yeah. I agree with you," the officer said with a nod, stunning Simon into silence.

Miranda appeared equally as surprised, but she found her voice first.

"If Simon is willing to build this fence, Kyle," she said, nodding toward the officer's full clipboard and slightly emphasizing his name, "then do you suppose he will be able to run his business as he sees fit?"

It couldn't be that easy.

Miranda was really reaching, and yet shockingly, there it was.

The officer was actually nodding in agreement.

Kyle's gaze returned to Simon. "You have a clean facility and your horse and your herding dogs look well cared for. Your barn could use a little bit of a spruce up, but I'm guessing you know that already."

"Nothing a coat of paint can't fix," Miranda affirmed enthusiastically. "Aren't his dogs wonderful? They are Australian cattle dogs from the very best stock. Simon breeds and trains them and then sends them to their new owners. He even has a waiting list with ranchers from several states."

Simon didn't know what was more surprising—that Officer Peterson sounded like he might go easy on him instead of hitting him with the gazillion notes on his clipboard, or that Miranda appeared so animated about the cattle dogs.

She'd really been listening to him when he'd explained his operations to her, even though he knew he'd probably gone into far too much detail because of his natural passion for his business.

Most people's eyes started glazing over at some point when he really got into his subject, but not Miranda. She actually sounded proud of his accomplishments. His chest swelled just a little.

"I'll tell you what, Simon," the officer said. "You put up the privacy fence along your south border and we'll call it good."

Simon stared blankly at the hand Officer Peterson thrust out at him.

The officer was ready to call it good—except

that it *wasn't* good. Simon didn't have the kind of cash lying around to build acres of a privacy wall.

What little money he'd had, he'd just given Miranda to help with the twins' upkeep. Twins meant two of everything—and even though she had her own money and the insurance payout, he wanted to contribute. He was a man. He wanted to do something concrete to help. If he could ease her burden, he would. The twins were the most important thing.

But the fence—

Miranda reached out and shook the officer's hand, as smooth as could be, rescuing Simon from what could have been an extremely awkward situation.

"Done," she said in an overly cheerful tone. "And thank you, Kyle, for understanding."

The officer held on to Miranda's hand, and her gaze, just a little bit longer than Simon thought was strictly necessary. Long enough to make Simon uncomfortable and feel like a third wheel.

"Can I take you for coffee sometime?" Kyle asked Miranda. "That is, unless…" He nodded toward Simon.

"Oh, no, Simon and I aren't together."

Simon clapped Kyle on the shoulder, refocusing his attention before he realized Miranda hadn't actually answered his question.

"Can I walk you back to your car?" Simon urged.

"No need." Officer Peterson gathered his clipboard and tipped his hat to Miranda. "I've got to get back to the station and fill out my report. You know how it is with police work. Endless paperwork, it seems like. Anyway, you get that fence built and I think our problem is solved. In the meantime, you two should enjoy this sunset. It's unseasonably warm weather this evening, don't you think?"

Officer Peterson didn't wait for an answer, but turned and headed back over the hill to where his SUV was parked. The sound of tires on gravel signaled the end of that particular confrontation.

And now Simon had a whole other one to face.

Miranda chose a chocolate chip cookie over a piece of fruit to assuage her sweet tooth, and turned around in her seat so she could view the lake.

The officer was right. It was a lovely evening.

Too bad she had to ruin it with the whole not-cashing-the-check nonsense. Simon had already had a stressful day, and now she was going to have to add to it.

Just what she didn't want to do.

For a moment she considered staying silent on the matter and tucking the check away somewhere for safekeeping, but that was only a temporary solution to a larger problem. Sooner or later Simon would realize she hadn't cashed the check, and then he'd have every right to come completely unglued on her.

No—it was better to be honest and up front about the check right out of the gate. Besides, he could probably use the money to help fund his privacy fence.

All the more reason for her to get this out in the open as soon as possible. Maybe it wouldn't be such a big deal after all.

Simon tossed his hat on the table and sat down beside her.

"I suppose I should thank you," he said in a voice as coarse as gravel.

"What?" Of all the things she thought he might say right now, that wasn't one of them, especially because he didn't sound particularly grateful. "Why?"

"Don't tell me you didn't see the way Officer Peterson was looking at you. Smart of you to distract him that way."

She must be out of practice, because she actually *hadn't* noticed. She wasn't in the market for a relationship, but she thought she'd know if a man was showing interest in her. Until Kyle had asked her for coffee, she hadn't been on that wavelength at all. Did Simon really imagine she would *flirt* with a peace officer to get out of trouble?

Or rather, get *him* out of trouble.

The nerve of the man.

"Well, thank you for working your charm on him. I was concerned there for a while."

"You're mistaken. This has nothing to do with me. I think Kyle admires what you're doing here at the ranch. He's just being nice, trying to help you fix the problem between you and old Mrs. Stanton."

"Hmmph. Being nice? *Kyle* was admiring *you*. He asked you for coffee."

If Miranda didn't know any better, she would have thought she detected a note of jealousy in his tone.

But of course that was ridiculous. Why would Simon care if another man found her attractive?

"Which I turned down," she pointed out.

He scoffed. "No, you didn't. You didn't answer him at all."

She clicked her tongue against her teeth. "Same difference. And honestly, does it even matter how it happened? The point is that we have a *solution*—and one that doesn't require any more interactions with Officer Peterson."

Why she thought she needed to reassure him on that point was quite beyond her understanding.

Simon lifted one eyebrow, then frowned.

"Not a *viable* solution."

She tilted her head and captured his gaze. "I'm not following. When you build the fence, your problems go away—and so does your nosy neighbor. The next time Blanche Stanton phones the police, they'll tell her to mind her own business."

"I don't—that is—" His face turned an alarming shade of red and he coughed as if he was choking on something.

She gave him three helpful thumps between his shoulder blades to dislodge his breath. Not exactly the Heimlich maneuver, but—

"I don't have the money," Simon mumbled, his voice so low that Miranda could barely hear the words.

She leaned in closer. "What did you say? I didn't quite catch that."

"I said I don't have the money to build the fence!" This time his voice was loud enough to be heard in the next county.

"You don't have to shout."

He growled. Literally, actually *growled*, and Miranda briefly wondered if maybe he was spending a little too much time with his canine companions.

"You don't get it, do you? You just put my head on the chopping block, promising Officer Peterson that I will comply with something that I don't have the resources to build. What's going to happen when that fence *doesn't* get built, huh? It won't just be Blanche breathing down my neck. My whole operation will be in jeopardy."

"I understand," she said. And she did—far better than he did right now. Because happily, she had the answer to his problem tucked away in her purse. He'd be so relieved that she intended to give him his money back.

Problem solved.

"Hold that thought for a moment."

She jogged back to her car and returned with her cute, high-end black clutch purse that was highlighted with a sparkling red rose.

"I have your remedy right here."

Laughing, she waved the purse under his nose. He frowned.

Of course he frowned. What else did Simon West ever do? She wanted to roll her eyes in exasperation.

But he'd be smiling in a moment.

"Ready?"

She snapped open the clutch and then paused for dramatic effect.

"Miranda," he warned with a growl.

"Oh, fine, spoilsport. Here," she said, pulling out the envelope he'd given her earlier. "This is the answer to your problem."

She tried to hand the envelope to Simon but he just stared at it, unmoving, his expression as hard as stone.

"That's for the twins," he said after an extended pause.

"Is it?" Miranda took the blank paper from the envelope, laid the check on the table and exaggerated her examining of both blank sides of the printer paper. "I don't see anywhere on here where this check is designated to the twins. No note or anything."

"You know well and good that's what it's for. Why else would I give you money? I didn't think I had to spell it out for you."

"You didn't. You don't. And I do know what you were trying to accomplish here. That's very sweet, and the twins and I appreciate it.

"But here's the thing—I don't need your money. I made a very good living as a celebrity photographer. A great one, actually. And since I'm really not the sort of woman to spend huge amounts on myself, I tucked most of that money away. I didn't know at the time I would be able to use it raising Harper and Hudson comfortably, but God knew."

Simon flinched but remained silent, his scowl still firmly set.

"And that's assuming I never use my photography skills again, which I can't imagine. Even without my savings, and even in a small town, I have a viable career."

He grunted. She didn't know which part of what she'd said upset him. Maybe all of it. But he should be thinking about his fence right now and not his ego.

"I've already set up investment funds for their college expenses. Their future is as set as their present."

She pushed the check in his direction.

"Keep your money. Build your fence," she urged.

He crossed his arms, and his jaw tightened until she could see his pulse throbbing at the base of his neck.

"There are lots of other ways you can support the twins besides using your checkbook," she said, trying to soften the blow to his ego. "You can be their male role model. You know how important that is. A man to love them and give them guidance."

He didn't so much as blink.

"What?"

"Until some other guy comes along."

Miranda wasn't going to get into this with him. There was no other guy, and she doubted there ever would be.

Simon was their godfather—an important influence in Hudson and Harper's lives. That wasn't going to change.

But there was no point in telling him that, because he wasn't listening. He'd completely turned himself off to her.

She sighed. "I really, *really* didn't want to have to do this, but it appears you leave me no choice."

Picking up the check off the table, she held the top corners between her fingers and thumbs and tore it neatly in half.

He stood so fast that Miranda was glad the picnic table was secured to the ground with concrete. It was a wonder the whole thing didn't crack into sawdust with the intensity of Simon's movement.

He stalked away, muttering under his breath and shoving his hair back with his free hand. Miranda couldn't hear what he was saying, but she suspected it had something to do with her, and they were probably not very nice sentiments.

Suddenly, he swiveled back on her.

"I'll write you another one. Maybe you don't need the money, but I want to do something concrete to support my godchildren."

She shook her head. He wasn't getting it. She could see that he wanted to give sacrificially, and she didn't want to stomp on his ego, but she had to make him see her point.

"I'll tear up any check you write. You can't win this battle, Simon. The best thing you can do right now is build your fence so you have a business to sustain you and you can keep rescuing your dogs. That won't happen if animal control shuts down your operation. The twins need you around as a role model, not a banker."

"But—"

"Nope. End of subject. Now, I'm going to leave you to your nice sunset and get back home to Hudson and Harper. When you figure out what you want to do, give me a ring. You have my number."

She couldn't help but smile the tiniest bit as she strode up the hill. Simon might not realize it right now, but she'd done him a huge favor, because the twins really did need their godfather in their lives.

Together, they'd find the answer to this dilemma. In the meantime, it was—

Miranda: one.

Stubborn Cowboy: zip.

Chapter Eight

The next Saturday, nearly a week after the incident with Officer Peterson, Simon was working on obedience training with some of the rescues he hoped to find forever homes for at the upcoming Christmas adoption event, but his heart and mind weren't in it and the perceptive pups could tell. They were all over the place, just like his thoughts.

He'd reached for his cell phone to call Miranda a dozen times, and a dozen times his thumb had strayed from the call button and he'd ended up pocketing his phone.

He'd never been so frustrated in his life.

Just when he was starting to like Miranda, maybe even admire her, she had pulled the rug out from underneath him, exposing his weaknesses and vulnerabilities.

He hadn't always been the nicest guy. As a

youth he'd floundered, because he had no foundation, no family to care for him. And he would do anything—anything—to make sure the twins never found themselves in a similar situation.

While he now conceded that Miranda may have been right about the money, he had his pride, and she had popped his male ego like a blade into a balloon when she'd ripped his check in half. He'd felt every tiny tear of the paper in his gut. His emotions had warred between humiliation and anger.

Even thinking about it now, a whole week later, made conflicting feelings swirl around in his chest like a whirlwind. He wanted to be the role model the twins looked up to. But even with his new faith, could he be that man? It seemed as if it was one step forward, two steps back in his life right now, especially since Miranda had arrived.

What could he offer the twins that Miranda didn't already provide?

And yet his concerns didn't negate his heart-felt conviction that he *needed* to contribute to the twins' well-being in a concrete way. Maybe he'd made a misstep with the check, but the reasoning behind his offering hadn't changed.

What had she said? That the twins needed his presence in their lives more than his money, a man to love them and give them guidance.

Lord, how can I be that man?

He needed a new game plan. Something that would work for all of them.

What he had to do, he realized, was make up with Miranda, set aside his pride for the sake of the twins. Be the one to step up and make the first move. If he and Miranda spent time together with Harper and Hudson, maybe they could find some common ground and learn to get along better with each other for the twins' sake. Certainly, there'd been moments when they'd worked together successfully, but those didn't outweigh the number of times they'd butted heads over issues.

He needed to find things they could do together. Events that Miranda, Hudson and Harper would all enjoy. Keep it light and friendly.

He hesitated a second before dialing Miranda, and that was only because he didn't know what kind of immediate reception he would get.

Would she hang up on him?

He snorted. What was this? High school?

He felt like a teenager phoning a girl for a first date, only in this case, he and Miranda were adults who'd gotten off on the wrong foot.

Several wrong feet, actually.

Of course she wouldn't hang up on him. Technically, he was the injured party here. But he was going to let that go for the twins' sake.

Surprisingly, Miranda answered on the first

ring, catching him completely off guard. He couldn't even stammer a hello.

"Simon. What's up? Is everything all right with the doggies?"

"The dogs?" Her question confused him for a moment. "No—yeah—the dogs are fine. I was just—"

He paused and cleared his throat, his nerves tingling from the tips of his toes to the top of his head.

"If you and the twins are free this afternoon, I thought we might take them to the Christmas carnival at church that the youth group is putting on. They do this every year and it draws most of the community, especially the children. They've got all kinds of little games and prizes, and the money goes toward feeding Christmas dinners to the homeless."

"I heard about that during church announcements last week and I was just bundling the twins up to take them."

Simon's spirit dipped.

"Oh. I see. Well—"

"But why don't we meet you there and we can hang out?"

He felt as if his heart was on a spring, popping back up again as easily as it had fallen.

"Yeah? That'd be—great." His throat tightened around his voice.

"Wonderful. See you there in twenty?"

Simon assented, then hung up the phone and headed for the house to wash up. As he splashed cold water on his face, he stared at himself in the mirror, for once taking stock of what he saw.

Debating on whether or not to change his shirt, he wet his hands and shoved his fingers through his curls, trying to tame them, but it was hopeless, and anyway, he had permanent hat hair from his cowboy hat. He ran his palm across his whiskers, wondering if he should shave, then scowled at his reflection and snorted.

Why should today be any different than any other day?

He was five minutes early from the time they'd agreed to meet, but Miranda's yellow convertible was already parked in the lot, sticking out like gold amongst coal. She really did need to get a more practical vehicle with all that money she'd said she had tucked away.

Miranda was waiting at the entrance with the twins in a double stroller. She waved as he approached.

"I thought since the carnival is interactive that we could leave the stroller out here and take the twins in together."

He grinned as he unstrapped Harper and pulled her into his arms. Together sounded good. Olive branches being extended both ways, it seemed.

With Hudson in her arms, Miranda gestured for him to follow her into the fellowship hall, which had been decorated almost as obnoxiously as Miranda's living room. Red, gold and silver garland everywhere. Wreaths at every booth, which were separated by tables.

"What should we do first?" Miranda asked. Simon wasn't sure whether she was addressing him or Hudson, so he merely shrugged.

"No deep-seated aspiration to throw darts at a balloon? I imagine it's quite therapeutic if you can pop one. And you get a prize."

"Shouldn't we walk around first?" he asked— not that he wasn't willing to display his dart-throwing skills. He had a dartboard at home and often spent evenings playing. It was one game a man could do without a partner or challenger.

Miranda assented and they walked through the aisles, taking note of the games aimed at the youngest children, and those more suited to adults. There was even a Wildhorn version of a kissing booth, where couples donated money to kiss under a sprig of mistletoe.

Simon made a note to avoid that booth. Trouble with a capital T.

Miranda slid her free hand into the crook of his elbow so they could stay together as they walked through the crowd. It was oddly comfortable, even with the curious glances that were thrown their direction.

"Cakewalk?" she asked, her expression eager with anticipation.

"For the twins? They can't even walk yet."

She laughed. "No, silly. For us. I mean, for us and the twins. We can carry them with us." She turned her attention on Hudson. "What do you say, Hudson? Think we can beat Uncle Simon and Harper?"

"So not going to happen, is it, darlin'?" he responded, directing his comment toward Harper, though his smile was for Miranda.

The cakewalk alternated between older kids and adults, so they had to wait their turn, but it wasn't long before they were on their spots, ready to begin walking with the music, which was, appropriately, a lively version of "Jingle Bells."

Even laden with the babies, both he and Miranda laughingly caught chairs through the first few rounds, and before he knew it, it was just him and Miranda left, fighting over one chair. His competitive nature reared and he clutched Harper to his shoulder.

"This one's for you, baby girl," he whispered.

Around and around they went. The inky-haired teenage boy in charge of the MP3 player took his time about shutting down the music, but when he did, Simon leaped for the chair, which happened to be facing his direction.

He hit the seat just as Miranda rolled around, squealing in surprise as she made contact with Simon's knee and not the chair. She tipped to the side, clearly going down, but she had the presence of mind to press Hudson into Simon's waiting arm. He'd been reaching for Miranda but had no choice but to take the baby instead.

His pulse ratcheted as Miranda landed in an inglorious heap. For a moment she didn't move or speak, and he wondered if she'd had the wind knocked out of her. She'd landed pretty hard. But then he heard her groan as she rolled to a sitting position, favoring one knee.

He was kneeling beside her in a second, but he was limited in how he could help her with two babies in his arms—babies who were both clapping and giggling as if they wished for Miranda to do it again.

Hudson in particular thought being suddenly tossed into Simon's arms was great fun. At least Miranda's fall hadn't hurt the little guy, and he had to give Miranda props for getting him to safety before impact.

Simon definitely didn't want anything like that to happen again.

"Miranda?" he asked gently. "What hurts, honey?"

She groaned again, her face flushing. The teenage boy running the music was at her side, a concerned look on his face as he offered his hand to her.

"Only my pride. And possibly my knee, although it's not anything major. I may have twisted it a bit as I fell."

"Can you stand?"

She nodded and slowly came to her feet, carefully testing out her left knee before putting any weight on it.

"Yep, good to go," she said as much to the crowd that had formed around her as to Simon.

"Are you sure?"

"Of course. And thank you," she said to the teenager, who beamed back at her.

His brow creased. She was taking this far too well.

He probably would have crawled into a hole and not come up again. Ever.

But not Miranda.

She smiled at those surrounding her and curtsied, as if she had just finished putting on a play instead of flopping nose down on the concrete floor.

Curtsied.

People actually started chuckling and clapping, offering their support, while all he could think about was that it was a wonder she *hadn't* hurt herself more than she had.

Just another addition Simon could make to his mental list of differences between them.

While Simon admittedly took everything too seriously, Miranda was—

The truth was, he didn't know how to describe her. Emotions swirled around and knotted themselves in his chest whenever he even thought of her. But one thing was for certain. They were as different as night and day—in the way they perceived the world, as well as how they encountered it.

Before he'd gotten to know Miranda, he hadn't realized what a strong and dedicated woman she was. He'd misjudged her. But now that they were spending time together with the twins, he had the distinct impression it would be harder than ever to be the godfather he wanted to be.

He and Miranda were so different. He didn't understand her view of the world, and before long, she would get tired of his cup-half-empty outlook.

He'd made a mess of every relationship he'd ever been in, and Miranda was a complicated woman.

Could they be friends? He had a hard time seeing through their dissimilarities, and he was nothing if not practical. The more time they spent together, the larger their differences appeared.

How long before the gap between them would be too far to cross?

Well, that had been humiliating.

When she was a kid, Mason used to tease her that Klutzy was her middle name. And she'd just proven that for the benefit of the entire town.

And Simon.

At least she'd provided a good laugh, after everyone was certain she hadn't actually injured herself in her inglorious fall. And the twins had loved it. They thought it was all a game, which was just as well.

Her knee hurt slightly but not enough to make a big deal of. She'd ice it when she got home. In the meantime, there were plenty of other booths to explore.

Simon threw three darts, popping the same number of balloons, and won a purple giraffe for Harper. He then proceeded to knock down bottles with a tennis ball and won Hudson a large red ball with white stars on it.

Miranda was glad for that, because she couldn't throw darts or tennis balls. She and Simon encouraged the twins to throw bean bags into buckets, which neither of them managed to do, not that it mattered. They each received small participation prizes—candy cane tree ornaments that the teens had fashioned into reindeer using pipe cleaners.

By the time they'd nearly finished visiting all of the booths, Miranda's knee was beginning to hurt in earnest, but she didn't want to cut the twins' fun short and Simon legitimately appeared to be enjoying himself for a change.

There were only two games left—the kissing booth, which Miranda was purposefully avoiding, and she suspected Simon was doing the same, and a big tin barrel filled with water and floating rubber ducks.

"Pick a duckie, win a prize," said the teenage girl, a pretty blonde with her hair pulled back in a ponytail.

"That sounds easy enough," Simon said, setting the giraffe on the counter and bracing Harper so she could lean over the barrel and grab a duck.

Harper being Harper, she tried to pick one for each hand.

"Easy does it," Simon said, gently returning one duck to the pond.

The teenager looked at the bottom of the duck, where the prize had been written in permanent ink, and handed Harper a six-inch dolly.

Simon shot Miranda a grin. "I'm glad we're getting to the end. I'm out of hands."

Miranda laughed and set the red ball on the floor so Hudson could have his turn at the duck-ies. His hand hit the water palm down, splashing it into Miranda's face.

She sputtered. "That's not how this works, buddy."

Taking his hand, she guided him to a duck, which he pulled out in triumph before it went straight for his mouth. Miranda was so busy trying to remove the duck without causing Hudson to wail that she didn't immediately see what Hudson had won.

The teenager stood with her arm stretched out, bearing a bag half-filled with water, a goldfish nervously swimming back and forth in its depths.

A real, *live* goldfish.

"Oh, dear. I don't—can we get something different?" she stammered.

The teenager shrugged. "Sorry. All we have left are dolls and goldfish."

Simon nudged her shoulder. "Come on, be a sport. As pets go, goldfish are a piece of cake."

Miranda cringed. "Says you. Remember the cactus? I have no idea how to take care of a goldfish."

"Don't worry. I'll set you up and show you the ropes."

That was what she was afraid he was going to say. Reluctantly, she accepted her live fish offering, but only because both of the twins appeared fascinated by it. They'd probably enjoy watching the fish, for as long as that lasted.

"I think we're finished here," she said, eyeing the ball at her feet. "But I can't pick up the ball and hold the fish at the same time, and you've got your hands full, too."

Mason appeared at her side, his mischievous brotherly grin causing Miranda some pause.

"I'll help with the ball and the fish," he said, picking up the ball, taking Miranda by the shoulders and pushing her *away* from the exit. "But you've missed one booth."

"Knock it off, Mason," she said under her breath. "I've been embarrassed enough today."

"Yeah, I heard about your little fall. Are you sure you didn't hurt yourself?" At least he sounded semiconcerned, though no less impish.

Big brothers. Can't live with them, can't shoot 'em.

"Nothing an ice pack won't fix," she assured him, not that Mason was going to listen.

Unfortunately, Simon was following them, probably not realizing he was a lamb being led to the slaughter. He really ought to know better, having been best friends with Mason for over ten years.

"Nothing that a little kiss can't fix," Mason amended, shoving Miranda underneath the mistletoe in the kissing booth.

"I don't have any more cash," she protested.

Mason grinned like a Cheshire cat and tossed the teen behind the table a five-dollar bill. "It's on me. Simon, the honor is all yours."

Simon eyed the booth—and Miranda—dubiously. He looked like a kindergartner, afraid of getting cooties. Miranda didn't know whether to laugh or be offended.

She chose laughter.

"A kiss to make it better," Mason prompted.

"Am I really that bad?" Miranda teased, handing Mason the goldfish and shifting Hudson to her right arm so she could offer Simon her left cheek.

"Yes. I mean no. I mean—" Simon stammered, looking like a deer caught in headlights.

Miranda raised her brows. "Is it yes or no? There'll be a foot of snow in Texas before you figure this out."

Simon scowled, intensely concentrating, clearly looking for a way out of this situation, and that only made Miranda and Mason laugh harder.

At length, he tipped his hat back with the arm that held the giraffe and dolly and sighed, the poor, long-suffering cowboy.

He first pressed a kiss on Harper's forehead, then stepped forward and kissed Hudson, as well. Last, he leaned toward Miranda, his lips hovering over her cheek as if in indecision.

But when his warm lips finally met her skin, it wasn't the hasty peck she expected.

He lingered.

Chapter Nine

Simon's mind lingered on that kiss far longer than it should have. Stupid Mason for making a complicated relationship even more thorny. Kissing Miranda reminded him once again that she was a woman, and not just the twins' guardian.

Part of him wanted to do what he always did when threatened—fight. Fight the feelings, and stay far away from Miranda Morgan. Or was that flight?

Instead, he called and made arrangements for them to take a day trip to the zoo. At least the zoo didn't have a kissing booth. In fact, it was specially decorated for the Christmas season, with zoo lights in the shapes of animals. The kids would love it, and it would be the perfect place for him and Miranda to walk on neutral ground—literally and metaphorically.

Something told him the zoo was a place that

not only the twins would like, but that Miranda would delight in, as well. Anyone who enjoyed making play tents out of sheets would enjoy seeing all kinds of exotic animals. And he didn't even want to get her started on special Christmas decorations.

When he arrived at Miranda's cabin and rang the bell, she only opened the door a crack and poked her head out.

"We're not quite ready yet," she murmured, and then shut the door in his face.

He didn't have to see what was going on to be able to imagine the scene from the ruckus he was hearing inside.

Squeaking and squealing and shrieking and giggling—and not all coming from the nine-month-olds.

It must be total chaos in there. He waited patiently for a couple of minutes, but finally, his curiosity got the best of him and he slipped inside the door.

Miranda squeaked when she saw him.

"If you can just hold on a moment more, Simon. I have to put these two in the bath before we go. We were making hard biscuits for snacks and a certain someone—" she coughed the name "Hudson" into her palm "—had both fists in the bowl the moment my back was turned. He got flour and sticky dough everywhere."

"Maybe if you hadn't left the bowl on his high chair where he could reach it," he suggested with a chuckle.

She laughed. "You're right. My bad."

Once again his opinion of her shifted, bumping up a few more notches. It took a brave soul to attempt to make homemade anything with two nine-month-old babies "helping." That sounded like way more trouble than it was worth to any sane person, but Miranda was all smiles and laughter.

The house smelled scrumptious, but her kitchen looked like a powder keg had blown up in it—a keg of *flour*. Sticky dough dotted the counter, and Simon suspected more dough had gone onto baby skin than had made it into the biscuit batter.

To his amusement, the goldfish Hudson had won at the Christmas carnival was swimming around in a bowl on the far end of the counter. Miranda had managed to keep the little fish alive for a week.

"Can I help?" he asked, thinking he could wipe down counters or mop the floor or something useful.

Miranda grinned at him. "I thought you'd never ask. Can you grab me a couple of bath towels?"

He grabbed the towels—bright yellow, surprise, surprise—and followed her into the bathroom, stopping short as he entered.

The woman had an evergreen wreath in her bathroom.

In her *bathroom*.

And the toilet seat was decorated as Santa Claus. No shortage of Christmas cheer here.

Shaking his head, he turned on the bath water while she divested two wriggling babies from their dough-covered fuzzy footie pj's.

"This is so much easier with a second set of hands," she gushed. "Usually, my bathroom looks like a water bomb exploded in it when I have to give them a bath. These kids really know how to make a splash."

As if to prove Miranda's words, Harper started wildly kicking both legs, sending a wave of water over the side of the tub and utterly soaking one leg of Simon's jeans.

His gaze met Miranda's. She was desperately going for a mortified expression, but he could see she was barely holding in her mirth.

She shouldn't be laughing at him.

And he ought to feel affronted. Would have, in the past. But oddly, he could see the humor in the situation.

It *was* funny.

He chuckled and the dam cracked.

Miranda clapped a hand over her mouth and began laughing uncontrollably, holding her stomach and rocking back and forth.

"Oh, Simon. Your face!"

"You're one to talk." He reached over and wiped his thumb across her cheek where a large smear of dough remained. "It looks like you three are wearing more dough than you baked."

"We learned fractions today," she informed him with a mock snooty sniff.

He lifted a brow. He didn't know the first thing about children, but wasn't nine months a little young for a baby to be learning math?

She snorted when he tipped his head and stared at her in confusion.

"One fourth of the dough gets on your clothes, one fourth goes on your face, and if all goes well, half gets into the oven."

"You learn something new every day."

"See? I'm a great teacher, aren't I?"

He definitely learned something new every day when he was around Miranda. She was teaching him loads without a classroom and never ceased to surprise him. Sometimes good, sometimes not so good, but always something different. He handed her one of the towels and slung the other one over his shoulder.

"I have a much higher learning curve than figuring out only one new thing a day," she informed him as she soaped down the two squirming babies and then scooped Harper into one of the plush, vibrant yellow towels. "I learn several *hundred* new things a day, usually by trial and error. Mostly error."

"I noticed you like yellow," he observed.

"Why wouldn't I love it? It's the color of sunshine."

Yellow wasn't just Miranda's favorite color. Miranda *was* yellow. Sunshine. Tulips and daffodils and other spring flowers. She was always so quick to move on from whatever conflicts they had. She didn't hold a grudge and just let go, rising new with every morning.

He was more like midnight.

Dark and broody.

Which meant what? Was *he* the instigator of conflict?

He didn't want to be that man. Not when he'd worked so hard to do more, to be different from the youth he had been.

He sent up a silent prayer asking God for assistance to be a new and better man. Without the Lord, he was nothing.

As he lifted Hudson from the tub and wrapped him in an identical yellow towel, he mentally resolved to do better.

It didn't matter what his past had been, or even

if his natural predilection was to see the dark before the light.

If he could learn it, he could unlearn it, and hanging out with Miranda was as good a place to start as any. He'd never be bright like sunshine, but at least maybe he could reflect her rays.

"Let's take my new car to the zoo," Miranda suggested as they dressed the babies in identical outfits.

"You got a new car?"

"The safest SUV on the market," she said proudly.

"No tiny bumblebee convertible anymore?"

"Royal blue. Unfortunately, the SUV I wanted doesn't come in yellow."

He couldn't imagine why that new bit of information caused him a moment of dismay. It was a practical decision on her part, but it was almost like taking away a little bit of her personality.

"If you can get the twins buckled up in their car seats, I'll get changed into something more appropriate for the zoo. If I go in these," she said, gesturing to her dough-covered baggy golden sweatshirt and battered yoga pants, "the lions, tigers and bears are apt to want to eat me for lunch."

Even in a bulky sweatshirt with her shoulder-length chestnut hair pulled back in a messy bun, Simon thought the lions, tigers and bears weren't the only ones apt to notice her. She was a stunning woman. Any man would take a second look.

He shook the thought away. He wasn't here to date Miranda. He was here to learn to get along with her for the sake of the twins.

And even if that wasn't his primary motivation, there were dozens of reasons any attempt at a relationship with Miranda would be a disaster.

Fire and ice, for one. Sunshine and midnight.

That she was Mason's little sister, for another. There had to be something in the man code about not getting involved with your closest buddy's younger sister. Mason would have no choice but to take Miranda's side in a bad breakup and Simon would lose the best friend he'd ever had.

Was he willing to risk that?

And there was yet another wide chasm between them—even here in Wildhorn where she was the single mother of twin infants, in essence, she would always be the successful celebrity photographer with boatloads of money and a contact list full of famous friends, and he would still be the poor, simple country cowboy who could barely make ends meet, and whose existence was primarily working with dogs that would never have another chance at life were it not for him.

What sane woman would want that for herself? Especially because she came as a ready-made family. She would always have to put the twins first.

Not a chance.

He wasn't good for any of them.

The fact was, he had nothing to offer Miranda, or Hudson and Harper, so it was especially important not only for him to rein in any errant thoughts, but to also make it clear to her that he was in this for the twins and only for the twins.

"What about the kitchen?" he asked as Miranda slid behind the wheel and plopped a camera case in his lap. He felt guilty about leaving it such a mess, even if he hadn't been party to creating it.

She started up the engine and made a quarter turn in her seat so she could look him straight in the eye.

"What about the kitchen?"

"Don't you want to straighten it up a little before we leave? I should have offered to help," he said, although technically, he *had* offered to help.

"Zoo…messy kitchen. Zoo…messy kitchen." She paused and cocked her head as if deep in thought. "Nope. No contest. The zoo will win every time. Sticky dough can wait. I want to see the monkeys."

Simon probably thought she *was* a monkey. It certainly looked like a whole tribe of them inhabited her kitchen. And he had a point that she probably should have at least wiped down the counters before they'd left.

But she loved the zoo, and she knew Harper and Hudson would, too, especially with Christmas zoo lights. She couldn't wait to see their happy little faces all fascinated by the animals, hear the squeals and giggles when the polar bear swam by them.

And Simon—he'd made the first move, not once, but twice now, reaching out to her with a hand of friendship.

How great was that? She wasn't about to turn his overture away.

Hanging out with Simon was an adventure, to say the least, sometimes up the path, sometimes down. But even though it seemed like they often bumped heads, whether on purpose or as an accident…this was the *zoo*.

What could go wrong at the zoo?

She turned the corner and headed toward Tumbleweed Avenue, Wildhorn's version of Main Street. Running east and west, with only two streetlights at either end of the town, it was the primary shopping thoroughfare, such as it was.

About two blocks away from Tumbleweed Avenue, Miranda's SUV came to a sudden stop behind a long line of other cars. It appeared there was some kind of commotion on Tumbleweed. It wasn't like Wildhorn to have a traffic jam, and it wasn't a holiday, so there shouldn't be anything blocking the road.

"I'll go see what all this fuss is about," Simon said before hopping out of the cab and striding down the street.

He returned minutes later, a frown creasing his brow. Miranda hadn't been able to move her SUV an inch, and now there was a line of bumper-to-bumper traffic behind her, as well as in front of her.

"Are we missing a Christmas parade?" she asked, even though she knew from Simon's expression that it wasn't anything as nice as that.

Ever since the moment Simon had exited the SUV, Miranda had been praying there hadn't been a terrible accident on the road. She'd rolled down her window, and while the murmur of voices was quite loud, she didn't hear any sirens.

Simon didn't bother answering her teasing question.

"Those kids—the ones who messed up the Nativity scene at the church? They've struck again, this time out on Tumbleweed."

"Really? What did they do this time?" Despite Simon's grave expression, she was more curious than worried. She hadn't thought the Nativity scene was such a bad thing. Not the way Simon had.

"It's town pickup this weekend. Folks are encouraged to bring out their bags of late fall leaves and the town disposes of them for free."

"Right. I remember hearing about it on the news. The drop-off spot is in front of Duke's Hardware, as I recall."

"Well, it *was* in front of Duke's Hardware. Now it's the whole length of Tumbleweed Avenue. And it's an enormous mess."

"What do you mean?"

"Some *kids on a lark* dumped all of the leaves out of the bags and spread them from one end of town to the other. It's a huge disarray and it's got to be cleaned up as soon as possible because of traffic. As it is right now, no one can get through."

He pressed his lips into a grim line. "I'm sorry, Miranda, but the zoo is going to have to wait for another day."

"Of course," she immediately agreed. "Did you see what's being done to take care of the problem?"

"Lloyd Duke is handing out rakes and donating new lawn and leaf bags, and the townspeople have banded together to pitch in and clean up the mess."

Miranda glanced in the rearview mirror. "Well, this vehicle isn't going anywhere in the near future. Why don't we bundle the little ones up in the stroller and see what we can do to help?"

"Why am I not surprised?" He shook his head.

"About what?"

"That you'd want to pitch in, even though you have two active babies to look after. You amaze me. Hudson and Harper are just a natural part of your life. They don't slow you down at all."

"Why should they?"

He shook his head again and helped her unload the twins. The stroller became cumbersome as they hit the main street, which was covered with at least two inches of golden leaves.

Miranda gasped audibly at the sight. Multiple tones of reds, oranges, yellows and golds mixed to make the avenue look like the road leading to the gates of heaven. It was an absolutely beautiful sight to behold, leading from the far end of town all the way up to the life-size Santa's sleigh and wire-cast reindeer. Snow might have fit the theme better, but given that they were in Texas, golden leaves were a decent runner-up.

"What?" Simon asked, concern lining his tone.

"Can you watch both kids for a moment?"

"Well, sure, but—"

She was already dashing away, heading back to the SUV, where she'd left her camera bag.

She gently pulled the camera out of the case and quickly added one of the longer lenses, glorying in the feel of the weight in her hand as she slid the strap over her head and around her neck.

She took photograph after photograph of the leaf-lined street, along with pictures of the Christmas-light-decorated windows on most of the business storefronts, blinking holiday goodwill.

To her dismay, she realized she hadn't taken a single picture of the twins since she'd arrived in Wildhorn. It was all she could do to manage the care of two babies without trying to photograph them, as she should have done.

What had she been thinking? The twins grew and changed every day. She should be documenting it. Not to mention all the cute shenanigans they got into. Sticky dough pictures would have been adorable.

Well, she couldn't change the past, but going forward, she'd be taking such a variety and number of pictures of Harper and Hudson that everyone she knew would get tired of her showing them off.

She chuckled lightly. She sincerely doubted anyone could really get tired of seeing photos of that kind of cuteness.

She was short of breath by the time she returned to Simon's side. He started to ask her why she'd run off in such a dither, but she anticipated his question and lifted her camera.

"I wanted to document this, and my professional camera catches the light much better than my cell phone."

Simon nodded. "Great idea. I'm glad you think like a photographer. I would never have thought of visually documenting the crime scene, but it makes perfect sense to do so."

"Crime scene? What crime scene? All I see is leaves. A wonderfully colorful road of multicolored leaves."

"You don't think the culprits should be caught and taught a lesson?" he asked, sounding astounded that she couldn't see his point of view.

She could. She just didn't agree with it.

"At the very least, they ought to be given community service—picking up the trash by the side of the road for a hundred hours, since they made such a mess of it."

"This prank seems harmless enough. No worse than the Nativity scene, except that we'll have to clean it up. At worst, drivers will need to reduce their speed through the town, which in my opinion they ought to be doing anyway."

"And the townspeople have to stop what they're doing to clean up the mess." Simon held up the rake someone had passed him. "Doesn't that at least score them down for inconvenience?"

He sounded annoyed. Hopefully not with her, although she wouldn't be surprised if he was.

Miranda saw the scene completely differently than Simon did. She looked around and saw neighbors helping neighbors, all working together—some raking, others holding open bags in which to deposit the leaves.

Simon was right about one thing—people had had to change their plans. There was no easy way of getting through on the road until the leaves had been cleaned off it, and someone had to stick around to clean up the mess. The zoo was up in smoke for them today.

But the zoo would still be there tomorrow.

And as with the Nativity scene, Miranda was awed by the artistic workmanship of the pranksters who had strewn the leaves on the avenue. They weren't randomly dumped around, making messes of sidewalks and decorated storefronts, as she expected vandals would do.

No. It was meant to be a golden road. Miranda was sure of it.

She snapped a few more pictures and showed them to Simon.

"Don't you see the beauty here?"

"Don't you see the damage?" he barked back.

She snorted. "I wouldn't call it damage. It's just leaves. No person or property has been hurt by them."

"That depends on your definition of *hurt*, now doesn't it? The twins didn't get to go to the zoo today because of these vandals. I would call that direct damage."

"How do you know it was the same kids as the

crèche, anyway?" she asked, although she suspected from the care and artistry that had gone into the project that it was the same group of teenagers.

"They tagged it." He pointed to a macramé-like rope dangling from one corner of the Duke's Hardware sign. "Triple H. Just like the last time."

"I wonder what it means."

He shrugged. "Trouble."

Miranda took Hudson out of the double stroller and plopped him down in the middle of a fresh pile of leaves.

"Look up here, buddy," she coaxed as she took snapshot after snapshot of the bouncing baby boy.

"Can you grab Harper for me?" she asked. "I want to do some single photos with her, as well, and then get some of the two of them together."

"I thought you were documenting the damage," he said as he got Harper out of the stroller and set her down next to Hudson.

Miranda sighed. "There is no damage, Simon. Not really. I was taking pictures of the golden road. Besides, if I have to document something, I'd much rather document people. There's a reason I was a celebrity photographer and not a landscape artist."

The twins were giggling and pelting each other with handfuls of leaves, and Miranda continued to photograph them, as well as taking pictures of others cleaning up the stretch of road.

Neighbor chatting with neighbor. Children taking running jumps into piles of leaves and happily undoing all the work the laughing adults had accomplished. The church youth worked as a group, methodically gathering bags of leaves and placing them back in front of Duke's Hardware while elderly neighbors looked on.

Not only had it become a community event, but it also wasn't long before Miranda found herself the center of attention. Folks were interested in the way she went about snapping pictures of them with her professional camera, and before she knew it, she'd promised at least a couple of dozen people that she'd get business cards made up as inquiries came in for weddings, pregnancy pictures and family photo shoots.

"That was the fastest, easiest business start-up I've ever seen." Simon appeared particularly pleased by that statement. He actually smiled as he crouched by the twins and showered them with leaves.

Then he looked up at her and frowned. "But you don't need the money, right? So why are you giving all of those people false hope?"

"It isn't about the money. I love photography and I miss doing photo shoots. Up until today I didn't realize how much."

"It's something you can do on your own time, as much or as little as you want, to fit your schedule with the twins."

"Exactly."

He smiled again.

She would never figure out this man.

"I can guarantee you that you'll have more business than you'll know what to do with, but it's all country around here. Won't you miss the glitz and glamour?"

Miranda dove for Hudson as he stuffed a handful of leaves into his mouth.

"Oh, pah, pah, pah! Spit it out! Spit it out!"

Hudson wailed in protest.

"Blech. Blech." She forced her finger into his mouth and scraped out the remaining foliage.

Simon tossed down his rake and snatched Harper out of the leaf pile before she could mimic her brother.

"Oh, gross, Hudson," Miranda groaned.

She'd thought she'd been doing better, getting a handle on the whole motherhood business, but every time she gave herself a pat on the back for a job well-done, something like this happened.

Maybe she really *was* the lost cause Simon seemed to think she was.

Her gaze reached his, but instead of the judgmental frown she expected, he held up his free hand in surrender and burst into laughter.

"What? I didn't say anything," he said when she lowered her brow.

"You didn't have to."

"You were the one who told me kids were gonna put stuff in their mouths that they weren't supposed to."

"Yes, but not an entire fistful of leaves."

"You should have gotten it on your camera for posterity's sake. You could have teased Hudson with it when he was a teenager."

"I was too busy trying to get the leaves out of his mouth." Miranda scooped Hudson into her arms.

"In you go, you little scamp," she said, strapping him back into the stroller. "And somewhere," she continued, digging through the designer purse she was currently using as a diaper bag, "I think I've got a package of crackers for you to nom on. It's much better tasting than leaves, I promise you."

Simon didn't immediately put Harper in the stroller with Hudson. He appeared to be waiting for something.

Oh, yes. The answer to his question.

In the whole panic of Hudson stuffing leaves into his mouth, Miranda had almost forgotten what Simon had asked.

"Will I miss the glitz and glamour of Los Angeles? Honestly? No, not really. I never did care for life in the limelight, even if it was mostly behind the scenes. I miss some of the friends I made out there, of course, but that's to be expected. I loved traveling, seeing new places and experiencing different cultures. But I've been there and done that, and as great as it was at the time, as Dorothy said, there's no place like home. Especially now that I have Hudson and Harper with me to love and to make my life complete."

Well, almost complete. Her life was full to overflowing with the twins, but she was suddenly aware of a tiny aching deep within her heart, something she hadn't noticed until the past few weeks.

He stared at her, taking her measure. He opened his mouth as if to say something and then closed it again.

"What?"

He shrugged as if he had no idea what she was talking about and then dropped his gaze, using his boot to leverage the rake back up to one hand. Still holding Harper, he busied himself raking leaves into a pile.

Whatever Simon had been about to say, the moment had passed now, leaving Miranda's imagination to fill in the gaps—gaps that zigzagged up and down and all around.

She'd always had an active imagination.

Chapter Ten

Simon marveled at Miranda's ability to see the good in everything. He'd looked at the street and had seen disaster, where she'd seen beauty.

And he supposed she had a point, although it had nothing to do with the prank and everything to do with the community.

Neighbors had gathered to help each other. Everyone from nine-month-old twins to Wildhorn's octogenarians had come together to make their town a beautiful place to live. Families were working as a unit. The church youth had jumped in to do their part. No one thought twice about chipping in to help.

This was why he loved living in Wildhorn. He knew what it was like not having a family. And he wouldn't wish it on anyone in a million years.

He kissed Harper on each of her soft, chubby cheeks and reluctantly returned her to her stroller.

Money couldn't buy what Wildhorn gave for free. And Miranda captured that through the long lens of her camera.

He wished he had more to offer her and the twins, personally speaking.

She had a wonderful network of extended family to support her. He wondered if she even realized how blessed she was. She had a faith in God that Simon envied. She didn't know what it was like to have no one—no family, no faith. To be knocked around by the world.

To be truly alone.

One thing was certain. He couldn't convince her that the work of these Triple H pranksters might eventually lead to something more serious. Something truly damaging, hurting people as well as property.

She looked through her camera lens and all she saw was light.

He just couldn't do that.

"It looks like things are pretty well in control here," Miranda said. "Folks are starting to get through. We'd probably better get back to my SUV now. I left it parked right in the middle of the street. People will be waiting for me to get out of the way."

"I'm going to organize a neighborhood watch committee," he informed her when they were buckled in and on their way back to his ranch. "I don't expect you to agree with me. I just wanted you to know."

He wasn't trying to cause another rift between them, so he was careful how he chose his words. Right now, more than anything, he wanted to get along with her—for the twins' sake, and also because, oddly enough, despite the fact that it drove him batty, he was starting to depend on her sunny outlook on things to keep him from sliding off the other end.

Her gaze flashed briefly in his direction.

"I think that's a good idea, actually."

"You do?" Whatever he'd imagined she'd been about to say, agreeing with him definitely wasn't it.

"I haven't changed my view on the whole thing. I still think it's just a bunch of harmless teenagers getting into some Christmas mischief—and they are artistic kids, at that. But I know there's a reason you have a different perspective and I want to understand where you're coming from, as well. I'm open-minded. I know you don't like to talk about what happened to you when you were growing up, and I don't want to pressure you to say anything you don't want to, but I would like to understand."

By this time, she'd pulled up in front of his house, but the twins were both sleeping and neither Simon nor Miranda moved to get out of the vehicle.

Simon inwardly balked. To say he didn't like talking about himself, and especially about his past, was an understatement. He didn't like to remember those times, much less dwell on them. He didn't like the person he'd been back then, the hotheaded kid life's circumstances had turned him into. But if he didn't speak now, she would never know why he was so adamant about the subject.

"I was a scrappy little kid. Skinny as a beanpole."

It was a start, but it was hard. Very hard.

She nodded but didn't interrupt his train of thought.

"The bigger boys, they picked on me a lot. It was about what you'd expect out of a group of bullies. I got a few black eyes. More than one awkward landing inside a Dumpster of decomposing food."

She wrinkled her nose.

"I know, right? So when puberty hit me in seventh grade, I started lifting weights. I was determined that no one was going to mess with me anymore.

"And they didn't. In fact, the guys who ruled the middle school recruited me into their gang. I was foolish and lonely, and I wanted to be accepted so badly that I didn't realize I was going to get messed with again, except in a different way."

Still, Miranda didn't speak, though her gaze brimmed with empathy and sorrow. She slid her hand across the cab and linked her fingers with his, silently giving him the courage to continue.

"Since I had no family, I desperately wanted to belong to something. I went right along with their hazing, allowing them to put me in all kinds of bad situations. But I didn't question it or complain about it.

"The first thing they made me do was dress up the school mascot—a big bear. I put a balaclava over his head and wrapped him in toilet paper. That wasn't so bad. I didn't get caught. The principal was mad, but all he had to do was take off the mask and TP and everything was back to normal. It wasn't like I permanently marred the mascot. Every student in the school had a good laugh and we moved on to other things.

"But then the next week they had me sneak into the school at midnight again, this time to tie pieces of string through the holes in everyone's locker handles so no one could open them the next morning. There were two hundred and sixty-five lockers—I still remember the exact number. It took me half the night, and I had two very healthy scares when the night janitor came around. My adrenaline was working overtime. But again—harmless, right?"

Miranda nodded. "Harmless, but not very nice. I've had a few experiences like that myself."

She paused. For a moment, it looked like she was going to say more about what had happened to her, but then she shook her head and closed her mouth. It felt as if she was waiting for him to say something to her, but he didn't know what he could say that would comfort her, so instead, he continued with his story.

"I doubled up the string on the lockers of the people I didn't like—the guys who used to pick on me. At the time I thought it was funny to watch them struggle to get their lockers to open."

He couldn't believe the depth of the narrative he was sharing with Miranda. Even Mason didn't know all the gory details.

But then again, Mason had never asked.

Miranda had.

"The next night I was supposed to siphon gas from some vehicles in a parking lot to fill up the tanks of a couple of the older guys' cars. I was having a hard time with it. Siphoning gas isn't as easy as it looks in the movies, by the way. Anyway, the cops showed up and the fellows I thought were my friends ditched me faster than you can say, 'You're under arrest.'"

"No. They didn't."

He groaned. "Let's just say orange isn't my favorite color, and I picked up a lot of trash on the side of the highway because of that one stupid move."

"Your friends weren't very courageous if they just deserted you."

"And it was stupid of me to break the law just to try to impress the jerks. They were never really my friends, but that's not something you realize until much later in life, when you can look back at it without all the emotions clouding the subject. Thankfully, soon after that I got sent to Wildhorn to live with the McPhersons. They were good to me. And I met Mason. His friendship is the real deal. I was still kind of a jerk for a while, but he pulled me out of the funk I was in and set me on the straight and narrow."

A shadow crossed her expression, but all she said was, "He's a good guy."

"Yes, he is."

"And now I understand why your view is so different from mine. I can see the obvious parallels between what happened to you and what's been occurring around here. Dressing up the bear and TPing it. But do you really think it's possible that Wildhorn has some sort of gang activity going on? That seems so unlikely to me, given what a small town this is."

He shrugged. "It could happen anywhere."

"Growing up, I don't remember much crime in Wildhorn at all, of any nature. I never even heard about thefts. No one locked the doors to their cars or their houses. I guess times have really changed."

Her brow knit in concern and he immediately backpedaled. He didn't mean to frighten her with his theories, only open her mind to the possibilities so she wouldn't take any unnecessary risks.

"Like you said, it's probably nothing," he amended, adjusting his cowboy hat lower over his eyes. "Kids on a lark, right? Nothing dangerous. Wildhorn is still one of the safest towns to live in—in Texas, or the whole country, for that matter. Our crime rate is remarkably low across the board.

"The police would already be involved if they felt there was a viable threat," he continued. "I'll organize an off-the-record neighborhood watch, something casual, just to keep folks alerted to the situation. The sooner we catch the culprits, the sooner the pranks will stop, innocent or not."

"I'll talk to Mason and Charlotte, and mention it to Pastor Corbit. It won't take long for the word to get around. Shall I have anyone interested in being involved call your cell phone?"

"That'll work. It's best if we can catch the pranksters red-handed. We need to get some cold, hard evidence so we can convince them to stop what they're doing. But in the meantime, I want you to take extra precautions for you and the twins. Lock your doors. Keep your cell phone on you. And put my number on speed dial."

"And this is only because of the leaves on the street?"

Her words could have been laced with sarcasm, but when he met her gaze, he realized she was teasing him, and he let out a breath that released the coils of tension in his neck and shoulders.

He wanted her to be serious about this, but not too serious. He didn't want Miranda to lose any of the open, trusting vibrancy that made her the woman she was. But he didn't want her to be in danger, either.

He'd protect her and the twins, no matter what happened. He'd keep his eye on her, but he didn't want her to feel hovered over, like she wasn't a strong, independent woman.

She was. No doubt about it.

He was just an overcautious man.

"Unless you have another reason in mind for putting my phone number on speed dial?"

Which sounded like flirting.

Miranda must have thought so, too, because her eyes widened almost as much as her gaping mouth.

Suddenly the path they were traveling on had

nothing to do with pranksters and everything to do with—

A place they could never go.

The next Saturday, Miranda was busy preparing the twins for the town Christmas party, her mind mulling over the last time she'd seen Simon. She had put his number on speed dial, but not because she was afraid of some random gang activity in the small town.

There was no gang. She was positive of that. Not in Wildhorn.

She understood why Simon saw things the way he did, and she was definitely aware of the striking parallels between his life and what was happening now, but that was his past, not Wildhorn's present.

She kept his number as the first spot on her contact list because—well, because she was starting to depend on Simon. For other things, not for his brand of protection. Even when they clashed, which was often, she still trusted that, while his methods left a little bit to be desired, he only acted the way he did because he cared.

About the twins, that is.

And lately, she wondered if he might even care just a little bit for her. She was hesitant to explore that thought, because she'd been so desperately wrong in the past when it came to relationships.

Which was why, even though she admired Simon and felt her heart jolt every time their eyes met, she was going to be very careful with him. Take it slow.

If there even was an *it*.

From the very first day they'd met again as adults, after she'd returned to Wildhorn to take up Hudson and Harper's guardianship, Simon's focus had been solely on the twins. As time went on, she and Simon had developed a friendship with each other, a bond she believed she could trust in.

She respected him.

But she was also wary.

She didn't want to get hurt again. He might not be the jerk who'd been so callous to her in high school, but she didn't trust her heart any more now than she had then. So Simon's number would stay safely on her cell phone and she would see where time and circumstance took them.

In the meantime, Mason and Charlotte were waiting on her.

She had a party to attend.

Wildhorn's community parties were nothing at all like the glitz and glamour of the functions she'd attended in Los Angeles, with catered food, professional string quartets and borrowed diamonds. There was no comparison whatsoever.

No—this small town *really* knew how to pull

out all the stops. The band was local, the food was potluck and the clothing anywhere from casual to Sunday best, all the better for dancing in. No one stood around in penguin suits holding flutes of expensive champagne. They were too busy Texas two-stepping.

"Is there anything cuter than dressing up babies at Christmastime?" she asked Hudson as she adjusted the adorable little red bow tie that matched the red suspenders holding up his black pants. She'd tried to slick back his thick tuft of chestnut hair with gel but all she'd managed to do was turn it into porcupine spikes that stuck out in every direction.

Harper, with her green velvet dress, was a little easier to groom. Her identical thick tuft of chestnut hair had been corralled with a big green ribbon on top of her head—a style Miranda had promised herself when she was a single woman that she would never do to her poor daughter. But with Harper?

Adorable.

"You two look delicious enough to eat," she told them, and then, amidst much squirming and giggling, she nommed on their sweet necks and tickled their tummies.

Miranda's camera was never very far away from her these days, and she shot several pictures of the twins next to the glowing lights of the Christmas tree, sitting back-to-back, or standing supported by foil-wrapped Christmas gifts. She'd seen some photo shoots with babies holding large ornaments or wrapped up in lights, and she wanted to make sure and take the time to do a full session before Christmas came and went. But right now they were in a hurry. Uncle Mason and Auntie Charlotte were already out in their SUV waiting for Miranda to follow along in hers.

But that didn't stop Miranda from admiring her children.

Were there ever any two more darling babies in the world? Miranda didn't think so. And she couldn't even begin to imagine her life without them now. They'd changed her whole world, and all for the better.

The cuteness, it hurt. They were going to be the life of the party.

Miranda had fudged a little bit with her own wardrobe, and she knew she was bound to stick out from the crowd, as well, but she reasoned that it was one of the few times she could even remotely consider wearing a cocktail dress, so she was all red sparkles tonight, even though she knew she would be overdressed.

She'd expected to catch folks' attention, all right, but she had no idea how much until she met up with her brother.

Mason's eyes widened to epic proportions

when he first caught sight of her, and his lips twitched as if he was holding back a guffaw, but Charlotte, dressed in a lovely pine-colored skirt with matching blouse, shot him a warning look and then linked arms with Miranda and told her how pretty she looked.

"She way overdid it," Mason murmured in Charlotte's ear. Charlotte pressed a cautionary finger over his mouth. Miranda wondered for the tenth time that hour if her dress was too flashy, but at this point she didn't have time to change.

When Miranda entered the church's fellowship hall where the party was being held, a hush fell over the room, followed by quiet murmuring. Every eye was on her, and it was only partially because of the two adorable babies she held in her arms.

She pretended to appreciate the decorations— columns wrapped like candy canes, red, green, gold and silver garland strung from the ceiling, and a gigantic evergreen in the middle of the room, glowing with lights and large bulbs and frosted with icicles.

"Told ya so," Mason muttered from beside her.

"Quiet, you," Charlotte reprimanded, swatting his arm. "Stop talking and help with the twins."

"I'm fine with them for now," Miranda said. Mason and Charlotte had their own brood to worry about, and she suspected many of the townsfolk would want to interact with the twins, which was her primary reason for attending the party in the first place. She could already see a swirl of movement headed in her direction.

"Honey, I think you're going to be way too busy to look after the twins tonight, and I really don't mind," Charlotte said. "And look—there's your mom and dad. You wouldn't want to deny the proud grandparents the opportunity to show off their sweet grandkids."

As Charlotte predicted, Miranda's mom wanted to take the twins for a stroll around the room, but Miranda's arms felt oddly empty without them, and she wasn't quite sure what to do with herself. She'd planned on having the twins with her for the whole evening.

She should mingle, she supposed. She hadn't had the opportunity to do that much since she'd returned to Wildhorn.

She sidled back up to Charlotte, who was straightening Mason's collar.

"The man can't dress himself," she teased mildly.

"If I had more than five seconds before being bombarded by children, maybe I could do a better job of it."

"You love being a daddy and you know it." Charlotte ran an affectionate hand across his stubbled jaw.

Mason grinned and shrugged, then placed a gentle hand against Charlotte's growing midsection.

"Dance with me, sweetheart?"

Miranda hadn't even noticed that the band had struck up a romantic tune.

"Go," she encouraged, waving them away.

"Your dance card isn't full yet?" Charlotte asked.

Miranda snorted. "No, I think I've pretty much scared off all the single men in Wildhorn with my over-the-top shimmer. I knew I had overdressed, but this—" she gestured to her dress "—is major overkill to the nth degree. There's not a single cowboy here who would dare to take me on."

Charlotte's eyes flickered with mischief.

"I can think of one." She nodded toward the door.

Miranda glanced back to see Simon entering with his foster mother on his arm and his foster father walking on the other side of him. Simon's head was tilted down toward Edith McPherson as she spoke to him.

He appeared relaxed and smiling, and Miranda silently thanked God that Simon had ended up in the McPhersons' care. From everything he had told her about them, they had significantly changed his life for the better.

She turned back to Charlotte. "You think?"

She wasn't nearly as certain as Charlotte seemed to be that Simon would display any interest in her. Not without the twins in her arms.

"I've never seen him so—*involved*—in a woman's life before you came along. He's a changed man."

"Yes, but that's because he's the twins' godfather."

Charlotte's eyes twinkled. "Is it?"

"You girls can gossip later. I want to dance." Mason made a face at Miranda and dragged Charlotte toward the dance floor.

Miranda crossed her arms, feeling suddenly very exposed and awkward, which wasn't like her at all.

She just needed to get over herself, she decided, heading toward the nearest group of people. Nothing that a little friendly chitchat with the neighbors couldn't fix.

Before long she was the center of attention the way she liked to be the center of attention—talking and laughing with a group of people.

A man's hand closed around her elbow from behind her and her heart leaped into her throat.

Simon.

Had he finally decided to ask her to dance?

She turned, a smile already forming on her lips, but it wasn't Simon staring down at her. Technically, no one was looking down on her at all. It was Kyle Peterson, and being as short as he was, he was staring up, his gaze full of blatant admiration.

Simon had accused her of using her charm on the officer last time they'd met, but she hadn't seen what Simon had seen.

This time, she did. Her heart sank.

"Officer," she said, trying to mask her disappointment. Instead, she sounded choked, like she had just swallowed a bullfrog whole.

"Kyle, please."

"You look different in plain clothes."

That was a dumb thing to say. She'd seen him out of uniform dozens of times before. He attended the same community church as she. But she'd never *noticed* him.

He tugged at his collar and cleared his throat. "You look—that dress is amazing."

"Er—thank you," she said, uncomfortable with the way he was complimenting her—and with his almost gawking perusal.

There was nothing wrong with Kyle, exactly. He was handsome in his own way, if a little short for Miranda's taste. He just wasn't her type—

Or maybe it wasn't so much that he wasn't her type as that she was comparing him to the one man in Wildhorn who *had* caught her interest.

She couldn't help that her gaze trailed around the room, following her heart as she looked for

Simon. She finally found him leaning against a post that had been decorated like a candy cane, wrapped in red and white ribbon.

He'd apparently lost his smile when he'd parted from his foster parents, because his expression now was as hard as stone.

She caught his gaze and smiled, hoping he would realize she needed rescuing and come ask her to dance.

No deal. He tipped his hat to her and his frown deepened.

She had the distinct feeling he was upset with her for some reason, though she couldn't imagine why. They'd parted on good terms the last time they'd seen each other.

But with Simon, it was always a toss-up. She ought to know by now that she could never gauge his mood. She'd never met anyone quite as unpredictable as he was.

"I was hoping to snag a dance with you," Kyle said, his voice rising. "We never did get that coffee."

"I—uh—" Reluctantly, she turned her attention back to Kyle. They hadn't gone for coffee because Miranda had never agreed to his request, although with the spark in his eyes, she wondered if he remembered it that way. Asking her to dance had caught her off guard, although she supposed it shouldn't have.

This was a party, and people were dancing.

Too bad the only man in the room she wanted to dance with was staring a hole through her back.

He wasn't going to rescue her.

Well, he could hang his stony expression on his beak.

She was going to dance.

"Thank you, yes," she told Kyle, feeling a little guilty when his expression lit up like the brightly decorated evergreen in the middle of the room. "I'd love to dance."

Chapter Eleven

Simon watched Kyle encircle Miranda's waist through narrowed eyes. He didn't move a muscle, afraid if he did, it would be to stalk over to where they were dancing and snatch Miranda out of Kyle's far-too-familiar arms.

"What are you waiting for, buddy?" Mason jerked Simon from his thoughts when he bumped shoulders with him.

Was it that obvious?

Granted, Mason knew Simon better than most folks did, but he hoped his admiration for Miranda—and his sheer frustration that she was dancing with any other man besides him—wasn't somehow being publicly broadcast through his expression.

That was all he needed—Mason razzing him about Miranda.

He shook his head. He wasn't going to give himself away that easily. "Waiting for what?"

"Oh, come on. Admit it. You have a thing for Miranda."

Simon cringed. His feelings for Miranda, as confusing as they were, were bound to come out sooner or later. He ought to be appalled with himself, although he couldn't quite find it in him to feel it as much as he knew he ought to be. He was tearing the man code into pieces and he didn't know how to stop it.

"I don't—"

"Charlotte and I have been observing the two of you doing this crazy back and forth thing for some time now. You're clearly attracted to each other. Wouldn't it be easier to just admit how you feel and go get what you want?"

That was half the problem. Simon didn't *know* what he wanted.

Not exactly.

Whenever he thought about Miranda, his insides started getting all twisted up and his mind…

His heart…

He groaned softly.

"If I did feel something," he said tentatively, "and I'm not saying that I do—she's your little sister. How do you feel about that?"

Mason chuckled. "I don't know whether you've noticed or not, but Miranda is all grown up now."

"I've noticed," he muttered, not quite looking Mason in the eye.

"Oh, I get it. You don't want to date her because she's my sister, and guys aren't supposed to do that."

"I never said I didn't want to date her."

Mason pumped his fist. "Then you *do* want to date her. Ha. I knew it."

"It's complicated."

Mason slapped his back. "Isn't it always, where women are concerned?"

They chuckled in agreement.

"There's women, and then there's my best friend's younger sister," Simon felt obligated to point out. "That is not the same thing."

"Look. I'm cool with it. I promise I'm not going to go all haywire on you if you have a relationship with Miranda, if that's what you're worried about."

"And if it ends badly?" Simon couldn't believe he was actually having this discussion with Mason. Saying it out loud made it real. "What happens then?"

"Will it?"

"I hope not."

"Then don't borrow trouble. Nothing is going to come between you and me. Our friendship is too important. But so is what you feel for Miranda. For all you know you could be watching her walking down the aisle to you before long."

Married men always wanted single men to get married. Simon thought that was because they wanted them to suffer in the same way.

At any time in the past, Mason's annoying statement would have sent him running for the hills. But now...

"And the twins," Simon added.

"What?" Mason looked puzzled.

"When I picture it, the twins would be walking down the aisle with Miranda. They are a package deal."

Mason grinned like the Cheshire cat and punched Simon on the biceps.

"Now, see? That's what I'm talking about. That's exactly why you're the right guy for her. You see Miranda and the twins as a package deal and you want it that way."

"Doesn't Miranda have a say in this? She might disagree with you on all counts."

"She doesn't. Disagree with me, I mean. I can ask her what she thinks of you, but I already know what her answer is going to be." Mason gestured toward the dance floor, where Miranda was dancing a second song with Kyle Peterson.

"Look at her. She's miserable out there."

Simon had to admit he thought so, too. They looked ridiculous together. Miranda was clearly uncomfortable. She would have towered over the animal control officer even if she wasn't wearing heels. Which she was.

She needed a taller man.

She needed *him*.

He was plenty tall enough for her, heels or no heels. She fit right into the crook of his shoulder as if she was made for it.

"That doesn't look right at all, does it?" Mason scoffed.

"No, it does not."

And Simon was aiming to fix it.

Now.

Miranda couldn't have been more surprised when Simon took her hand right out of Kyle's, twirled her around and whirled her away without a word of explanation.

One second she was in Kyle's arms, and the next she was in Simon's. She ought to be affronted by his alpha-man tactics, but really, she couldn't complain.

She *wanted* to be in Simon's arms.

"You probably should go apologize," she said.

Kyle was still standing in the middle of the dance floor, stunned into inertia.

Simon chuckled. "You're right. I probably should. And I will. Later. Right now I want to dance with you."

"Really? Because I got the impression earlier that you were unhappy about something. Something to do with me."

"Was I? I don't remember."

"Well, you were smiling when you came in the door with Edith, but when I saw you later—"

"You were talking to Officer Peterson."

Miranda's heart warmed when he didn't offer more of an explanation than that. He hadn't liked what he saw. He made it sound like the only *right* place for her to be was—

In his arms.

And at the moment she couldn't agree more.

She leaned her head against his chest and he tucked his chin on top of her head, drawing her close and swaying softly to the music. He was a good dancer, a natural leader and easy to follow. Which was good, since Miranda was not as coordinated.

She'd always felt awkward dancing. But not now.

She knew things were far from settled between them, and if they were headed toward a real relationship, they were both taking teeny-tiny baby steps, but right here, right now, she was in his arms, listening to the quick, steady tempo of his heartbeat, and everything was right in her world.

Who would have guessed that ten years after pining for a boy in high school, a young man who had laughed at her and brought her down, she'd be dancing with that very same boy, now grown into a rugged, handsome man whose angry youth was a thing of the past.

The feelings she'd experienced as an angst-ridden teenager paled in comparison to the way her heart expanded with the most tender of emotions now. Every nerve ending snapped and crackled pleasantly like a warm fire on a cold day.

"Lookee here." From behind her, some guy's hand stole out and made contact with Simon's shoulder, knocking them both off balance. He pulled her closer and swung them around to keep them upright.

"The cowboy and the celebrity chick. How do you rate, West? What did you have to do to get her attention?"

"Knock it off, Russell," Simon muttered.

"Just ignore him."

"Yeah," he agreed, but his tension was palpable.

"Thinkin' about marrying up? Like way, *way* up. She's out of your zip code, buddy," another man said.

"Mind your manners, Alfie Redmond," she scolded, but that only made Simon's jaw harden more.

"She's so far out of your league, pal. Wishful thinking."

Miranda didn't even know the third man. Why did they all have to gang up and pick on Simon? She knew he had to be extra-sensitive to being bullied, even if it was all in fun—and Miranda wasn't sure it *was* all in fun.

The guys, who all had women in their arms and were sorta-kinda dancing, had maneuvered around Simon and Miranda, making a circle and blocking them in, the jerks.

Simon stiffened and Miranda leaned back enough to catch his gaze.

Clearly the men's razzing was getting to him, but she didn't see why it should. Either these guys were all friends of his giving their buddy a hard time, or they were grown-up bullies. And Simon knew what to do with bullies.

"They're not worth it," she murmured.

What they were saying was ridiculous. In her eyes, she and Simon were perfectly matched. It wasn't as if she was better than him in any way, just because she'd been a celebrity photographer and he'd stayed here in Wildhorn to pursue his own dreams. She admired what he'd done with his life. There were many qualities about Simon she wished were part of her own character.

And as far as personalities went, Simon definitely held his own when they were together, even when they clashed.

And yet clearly he was bothered by the men's

words. Maybe it was thoughts of his past rising up to taunt him.

And all because of her stupid dress.

She now deeply regretted her choice of attire. She should have known better. Why had she ever wanted to wear a sparkly cocktail dress to a party in Wildhorn?

Because she didn't mind standing out in a crowd.

But Simon did.

"Don't you guys have anything better to do with your time than give us grief?" she asked, not quite able to keep the annoyance from her tone. "Your dates are going to abandon you if you don't pay attention to them."

Russell's date playfully slapped his chest. "That's right, big guy. After all this nonsense, I'm thirsty. Let's go find the punch bowl."

Russell laughed and let his date lead him away, and without him, the other two instigators danced their dates off in different directions.

Good. Well, that was settled.

Simon stopped dancing and stood stock-still, his muscles clenched tight.

"Men just never grow up, do they?"

She hoped her flippant observation would bring a smile to Simon's face, or at least unravel the coils of tension in his arms and shoulders, but instead, his jaw tightened with strain and his gaze grew hard.

"What is it?" she asked, wondering if he now regretted cutting in on her dance with Kyle. If he hadn't been dancing with her...

"It's nothing." He started rocking them slowly back and forth, but he was so tense that the movement was awkward and arrhythmic.

"Maybe we should just go," she suggested, meaning that they should leave the dance floor. Get a snack, or find the twins.

His expression lightened in relief. "You should stay. Have fun. But only if you're sure you really don't mind if I skip out of here."

"You're leaving the party?" she asked, confused.

"Isn't that what you just suggested?"

"No. I only meant—"

"They're right," Simon cut in.

"What? The men? Right about what?"

"You're too good for me."

She snorted. "That is about the most ridiculous statement I have ever heard come out of your mouth. This is about this outlandish dress. It's over-the-top and draws too much attention. I should have known better and I wish I had never worn it."

"It's not the dress. Although let me say you

are more beautiful than any other woman in the room."

"Thank you, I think. But I—"

She felt like she should apologize to him for something, but other than drawing attention because of the dress, she wasn't sure what that was.

Their gazes met and locked, and she reached out to him with her eyes, baring all the emotions she was feeling in her heart. His usual sea-blue eyes darkened like a tempest and his arms tightened around her.

Their attraction to each other was visceral. There was no way either one of them could deny it.

And she no longer wanted to.

"Simon," she breathed.

"Miranda, I—"

He dropped his arms to his sides, his fists clenching and unclenching, his breath coming in uneven puffs.

"This isn't going to happen."

It wasn't a definitive statement by any means. He sounded like he was trying to convince himself.

From her perspective, it *was* happening, and there was nothing either one of them could do to stop it. Their relationship was like a boulder let loose at the top of a high hill, gaining momentum as it tumbled down the side of the mountain.

Sure, they were polar opposites in every way, but if anything, that only made them stronger as a potential couple. He made up where she was lacking, and she liked to think she lent strength to him when he needed it, although she was clearly failing in that now.

He'd been through so many trials in his life. Surely a trio of overzealous testosterone-filled men wasn't going to trip him up from what could be a really good thing.

That wasn't the Simon she knew.

He was a fighter, a scrapper. He'd told her that himself. He stood up for what he believed in, and just now, when their gazes had met, she'd been certain he believed in *her*.

In *them*.

But then he was striding away from her with long, determined steps, headed straight for the door.

And he didn't look back.

Chapter Twelve

Simon hadn't run away because of anything the guys had said. He had *walked* away to give Miranda the opportunity to discover her freedom. To dance with other men and flutter around the room like the butterfly she was.

This was all about her. But he couldn't stand there and watch it.

He cared enough to walk away before their hearts became any more entwined than they already were. He'd felt the tug of his heart and the undeniable chemistry every time their gazes met, and he knew it wasn't all one-sided.

She cared for him, too.

Mason had encouraged the relationship. He might even have mentioned it to Miranda. But Mason was wrong.

And the guys at the dance, well, they were jerks, but they were spot-on.

Simon wasn't good enough for Miranda, and even more so because she came part and parcel with that beautiful set of twins.

He was just a poor, simple cowboy.

What could he offer her?

Nothing but his heart.

And while that might work out in romantic movies, this was real life. Miranda might have her own financial resources and not need someone rolling in dough, but—especially because of the twins—she needed a man with a strong, steady lifestyle, which was the furthest possible thing from Simon's constantly-walking-on-a-tightrope herding operation and canine rescue.

His dogs used to be enough for him, but now his heart had grown to make room for Miranda and the twins, and when they weren't there, he felt all empty inside.

But that was his problem.

Miranda would probably be happier with a man who smiled when he saw the sun rise, and she definitely needed a man with a firm faith in God's goodness.

Simon had been privately working on that part of it—cracking open the Bible Edith McPherson had given him when he graduated high school, and taking baby steps in the prayer department.

His prayers weren't anything formal. They were more like a running commentary with God while he worked with his rescues or groomed his cattle dogs.

When he'd sent his first tentative prayer heavenward, he'd expected it to ricochet right back down at him. Instead, he'd felt a quiet acceptance in his heart. No fireworks. Nothing he could put a name to, or share in words, but a sweet, silent something nonetheless.

He had yet to talk himself into attending a church service, but he figured that was probably the next step down the line somewhere. In the meantime, he just kept talking to the Lord, mostly about Miranda and the twins, because he had no idea what to do next where they were concerned.

A little divine guidance would be great. But since that wasn't likely to happen, Simon just kept to himself.

Mason had called on Tuesday to make sure everything was all right. Apparently, Miranda had taken the twins home not long after he had left. Simon felt bad about that. He hadn't meant to ruin the occasion for her.

He'd assured Mason that all was well, even though his life was far from it. He had hunkered down at his ranch and had spent the entire week putting the finishing touches on the training of the rescue dogs who would be taken to the adoption event.

Only a week and a half before the Saturday

event, and he still had so much to do—washing, grooming and making every pup look their best. Saturdays were always Wildhorn's busiest shopping days, even when it wasn't one week before Christmas. Of all the adoption events he sponsored during the year, Christmas was his best season. With a careful vetting of owners, a dog could be the perfect gift—one that would give years of love and joy to their forever family.

He was too busy to think about anything else besides the upcoming event—or at least that was what he'd told Miranda when she'd texted him about rescheduling the zoo.

The truth was, he didn't know how he was going to explain his actions at the party when he saw Miranda next, and he was dragging his feet because of it. He had to say something, but he didn't know what. He had answered her text with a cryptic one of his own, and from then on, he'd let her phone calls go to voice mail.

After a couple of days she'd stopped calling. He figured she'd probably given up on him. All the better for her.

But he was still the twins' godfather. He would have to face Miranda sometime, work things out and get over the awkwardness he was feeling.

Just not today.

He was elbow deep in soap suds trying to turn Zig and Zag back into the West Highland *white* terriers they had been before their most recent roll in the mud, when his phone buzzed in his back pocket.

It was probably Miranda again. He wished he had never insisted that she put his number on speed dial. She was punching that call button way too often.

At least this time he had a valid reason for letting it go straight to voice mail, and not just that he was pretending the phone wasn't buzzing at all.

But when his phone rang again five minutes later, Zig and Zag were towel dried and zipping through the house chasing each other.

Simon pulled his cell out and checked the screen.

It was Mason. No doubt calling to check up on him again.

Maybe Miranda had put him up to it.

He sighed and answered.

"Still fine," he said instead of hello.

"What?"

"I've been busy. I built an eight-foot privacy fence across my southern border, and the big adoption event is next weekend. That's why I haven't been answering my phone."

Wow. And how lame of an excuse was that? It sounded terrible even to him.

"I have no idea what you're talking about, buddy," Mason said.

"Oh." Simon had just assumed Mason was calling on Miranda's behalf. "What's up, then? Are the twins okay?"

"You should really be asking Miranda that question, but yes, the twins are fine. I'm calling about the neighborhood watch."

"Someone caught the pranksters?" he asked hopefully.

Mason paused. "Not exactly. They've, er, struck again."

Simon groaned. "What now?"

"You have to see it to believe it. They've hit Tumbleweed Avenue again, and this one's a doozy."

"Nobody saw them?"

"Not to my knowledge."

"How is that possible?"

"Search me. But you need to see it."

"I'll be there in ten."

"Can you do me a favor and call Miranda for me? I'm sure she's going to want to see this, too. And tell her to bring her camera."

Simon knew he was being set up. There was no reason Mason couldn't just call her on his own phone.

"Is it that bad?" he asked.

"Not exactly," Mason hedged again. "Look.

Miranda isn't at home and I'm not sure where she is, only that she has the twins with her."

"Yes. Yes. I'll call her. I'm sure she'll want to be there. She's part of the neighborhood watch."

A *reluctant* part. She was more likely to want to see what the *artists* had done.

He hung up with Mason and punched in Miranda's number. He didn't expect her to pick up, since he'd been avoiding her phone calls all week, but the phone only rang once before he heard Miranda's warm alto on the other end.

"What's up?" she asked cheerfully.

Why was it every time he thought she'd be upset with him—like right now, for example, when she *should* be ready to rake him over the coals—she surprised him with her positive attitude?

He sighed. She practically beamed sunshine. He had such a long way to go.

"Mason asked me to call you."

"Oh." Her voice dropped. He thought it might be disappointment.

"I'm sorry I didn't call you back earlier in the week. The adoption event is next weekend and—"

"You don't have to explain yourself. But I am kind of right in the middle of something. I'm taking pictures of the church youth group. They're waiting on me. So if you've got something to say, just say it."

"Where are you?"

"At the park. Why?"

"Apparently, the Triple H pranksters struck again."

"You're kidding. What is it this time?"

"I'm not sure. Something on Tumbleweed Avenue. Mason said to make sure you bring your camera."

"Okay. I'm just finishing up here. I'll meet you on Tumbleweed."

"Are the twins with you?"

"Of course. Always."

Despite all the promises he'd made to himself throughout the past week, Simon's heart warmed at the thought of seeing his three favorite people again.

It was hopeless.

He was hopeless.

A lost cause.

He could no more stay away from Miranda than he could stop breathing.

Unless he moved somewhere far, far away.

Like Mars.

Miranda took a few more snapshots of the youth group under a large elm tree and then pulled them in for a meeting to let them know something had happened on Tumbleweed Avenue again and their assistance might be needed.

They responded as enthusiastically as they always did. Much of the youth group's time was spent doing service projects. They were always ready and willing to help.

As was Miranda.

She packed the twins up in her SUV and made quick time to the main street. Anticipating similar circumstances to the last time around, she parked a couple of streets down from the road, set up the double stroller for Harper and Hudson, and then set off on foot the rest of the way.

She was curious about what kind of prank had caused Mason to suggest she bring her camera, but mostly, she was just anxious to see and talk to Simon.

He couldn't ignore her if they were face-to-face, as he had done with her texts and phone calls. And she needed to speak with him urgently, because after much reflection, she thought she had figured out what had set him off so vehemently and caused him to leave the party in such a rush.

Well, she'd known what the problem was from the moment it had happened. But now she'd come up with, if not a solution, then at least a suggestion that would ensure they spent lots of time together *and* possibly help his beloved dog rescue to be even more successful than it already was.

She wasn't ready to give up on Simon yet, even

if he apparently was ready to give up on her and the twins. She couldn't wait to share her thoughts with him and see if his reaction was as positive as she hoped it would be.

As she turned onto the avenue, her mind was distracted with thoughts of how she was going to explain to Simon why they needed to work together, but as soon as she caught her first glance of it and looked around, she gasped in surprise.

Tumbleweed Avenue had been TP'd from one end of town to the other. Miranda couldn't even begin to imagine how many rolls of toilet paper the kids must have used.

But the work they'd done was breathtaking. Simply and utterly amazing. It must have taken them most of the night. How no one had seen them was a mystery.

No wonder Mason had wanted her to bring her camera. The teenagers had strung toilet paper from one old-fashioned lamppost to the next, all the way down the street on both sides, carefully twisting and mimicking garland. The poles had all been wrapped from top to bottom to look like candy canes. Above the doors of every shop and business were enormous, intricately tied toilet paper bows.

The entire avenue was the epitome of warm, blessed Christmas spirit. It screamed merry and bright, highlighting the already-decorated avenue and bringing it to new heights of artistry.

She focused her lens on the artwork and started snapping photos.

"At least this won't take as long to clean up" came Simon's deep, clearly annoyed voice from behind her.

"But it's beautiful. Surely, we don't have to wreck it yet. No one else seems to be in a big hurry to do so."

Simon picked off his hat and shoved his fingers through his hair.

"I have to admit this is pretty impressive. They went to a lot of trouble. But I can't help but wonder what's next."

Miranda realized that would always be the question with Simon—what was coming next and would that something be worse than the last time?

"I think we can gather from this project that these kids mean no harm to the town," she assured him.

Simon didn't immediately reply. Instead, he busied himself taking Harper out of the stroller and swinging her into the air, smiling when she squealed in delight.

"I've missed these little ones."

Miranda noticed that he didn't say anything about missing her.

But that was where her idea came in—making herself useful to him until they got over this bump in the road. Until he *did* miss her when she wasn't around.

"I've been thinking a lot about your adoption event," she started. "I want to help."

His gaze widened in surprise. "Yeah? How's that?"

"I think I may have come up with a new, possibly better way to advertise—not only for this upcoming event, but for the future."

"I have posters on all the public bulletin boards and in the windows of some of the shops."

"Do they have pictures of your dogs on them—or better yet, photos of dogs and children that suggest forever families?"

He shook his head, his gaze brightening with interest.

"Do you think that would help?" he asked.

"You know what they say—a picture is worth a thousand words."

"I can see where that would work," he said, but then frowned. "It's a little too late for this year, though."

"Well, if you would have picked up your phone…" she teased.

Even under the shadow of his stubble, she could see that his face stained red. "That was immature of me. I shouldn't have ignored your phone calls. I'm really sorry. I didn't know what to say. I wasn't sure how to explain why I left the party so suddenly."

"You don't have to explain anything. I get it," she assured him.

"You do?"

She nodded. "It's forgotten. And as far as advertising for this year's adoption event goes, I don't see why it's too late for us to do something about it."

"You don't?"

"You have a printer with a copy function in your office, right?"

"Yes, of course."

"Happily, technology has increased by leaps and bounds in the last couple of decades," she ribbed. "No, but seriously. It won't take me more than an hour to do a photo shoot of the adoptable dogs and put together new posters for you. Then we can canvass the area this evening. It's perfect timing, really."

"You can do all that in such a short time?"

"Of course."

"But why would you want to, after the way I've treated you, I mean? You say you understand, but really, there are no excuses for my bad behavior."

"Then I forgive you." She grinned at him.

"Just like that?"

"Just like that," she assured him. "Now, we

ought to get going. But I have to run by my cabin first."

"Why?"

"To pick up Christmas outfits for Harper and Hudson. They're going to be your Forever Family models."

"That's an awesome idea. Did I mention how wonderful you are?"

He embraced her and twirled her and the twins in their stroller around and around.

She'd never *literally* been swept off her feet before. She liked the feeling.

As he set her back on solid ground, she felt dizzy and off balance and she pressed her hands against his chest to steady herself. Their eyes met and his gaze darkened and dropped to her lips. His heartbeat pounded under her palm.

With infinite gentleness, he lifted his hand to frame her face and tip up her chin. He moved slowly, giving her plenty of time to respond.

And respond she did. When he tilted his head so his mouth was aiming for her cheek, she turned hers and met his lips straight on.

Surprise flashed through his gaze before his eyelids dropped closed and he slid his hand to the nape of her neck to pull her closer.

This time he clearly meant to kiss her on the lips, and he did—so thoroughly and wonderfully that Miranda thought she might have discovered a literal cloud nine.

Every thought, every emotion, every nerve, was in tune with his. She'd never felt more alive, more connected to another person. This was life in Technicolor and she wished she had a way to photograph her feelings and keep them forever.

"PDA much?"

Mason's laughing voice drifted slowly into Miranda's consciousness. "This ain't no kissin' booth. Now, granted, Charlotte and I thought y'all ought to figure this relationship business out, but in the middle of Tumbleweed when there's a crowd around? Really?"

"Go away, Mason," Simon said, his lips still hovering over hers.

Mason held up his hands in surrender. "Just sayin', Simon. It's a good thing you're kissing the photographer or your picture would be spread all over Wildhorn's social media by tomorrow morning."

Miranda would happily have taken that photo—*and* posted it on every social media account she had.

Simon groaned and pulled away.

He didn't like to be the center of attention, and she respected that, but she didn't care who was watching.

She wanted the whole world to know.

Chapter Thirteen

Simon held Hudson and Harper in his lap while Miranda decorated the miniature tree he'd just bought for this purpose. She hung little bulbs and strung red garland around it, then checked the lighting through the lens.

"I still can't believe you don't decorate for Christmas," Miranda said, putting a green hat on Hudson. His little Santa's helper suit and Harper's matching female elf would contrast nicely with Zig and Zag, the dogs Miranda adorably still thought of as *twins*.

"What would be the point? It's only me and the dogs, and they don't care that it's Christmas."

"Hello—Christmas spirit, where are you? What happened to getting in the mood for all things merry and bright?"

Simon snorted. "When have you ever known me to be merry and bright?"

But sitting here cross-legged with both of the twins on his lap and Miranda zipping around with unflagging energy and excitement, he thought he might be as close as he'd ever been to those feelings.

There was just something *right* about the four of them being here together. Next year he might even go whole hog—cut down a real evergreen and toss around some tinsel. And of course, he would hang a sprig of mistletoe, maybe a whole bunch of them, which he'd be pulling Miranda beneath as often as possible for a long time to come.

"This publicity campaign isn't just about Christmas," she commented, as if reading his thoughts.

He situated Zig and Zag, and then Miranda sat the twins back-to-back just behind the little dogs. She lifted her camera and took as many good shots as she could in the short amount of time she had before the twins started crawling away and the dogs got distracted.

"What do you mean, it's not just about Christmas?" he asked when she had a moment to hear what he said.

"I'm picturing this as an all-year-round solution. Photographing one or both of the twins with each individual dog. You don't have a website, do you?"

"I'm not much of a computer guy," he admitted, feeling once again like a simple cowboy living in a world far too small for a woman like Miranda. "Forever Family has a social media page, but there aren't many pictures on it and I don't update it very often."

"Well, there you go. We take cute pictures of the dogs and the kids and get them up where people can see them. If we update the website and social media page every time you get a new dog, I think you'll see a real uptick in your rescue efforts."

"And you'll be the one taking the pictures?" He held his breath as he waited for her answer.

She laughed. "Unless you want someone else to do it."

Simon didn't want *anyone* else. And he was beginning to imagine how this might work out after all. Miranda could take pictures of the dogs and help him with the rescue. He could care for the twins when she had photo shoots to do.

Was the inconceivable possible?

Because there had been all kinds of possibilities in their kiss.

"I'd like to get a couple of shots of the twins with Chummy," she said. "I know he's your dog and he isn't going to be up for adoption, but I would love for the world to see how much you care about even the wounded animals."

She'd just given him a solid opening to say what was on his mind.

Speaking of caring…

Miranda, I care for you.

I want you and the twins to be part of my life.

But the words wouldn't come. They got all tangled up in his head and never made it to his lips.

He sighed and whistled for Chummy.

The photos of the twins with Zig and Zag had turned out even better than Miranda had expected, and it was a simple matter for them to make and distribute the posters.

She spoke to a lot of people as they canvassed. Simon, not so much. As usual, he turned introspective when there were others around. But that was okay. She talked enough for the both of them.

She supposed that was another way she could help him with his rescue efforts—spreading the word with, well, *words*. Maybe the Lord had given her the gift of gab for a reason after all.

As a surprise for Simon, she'd blown up the photo of the twins with Chummy into an extralarge poster and had added the Forever Family logo in big letters. She thought they could use it for all of the adoption events and then in between events he could hang it on his office wall.

There was another thing, also, that she'd noticed when she'd been going through her snapshots, although she hadn't shared the information with Simon yet—and wasn't certain she should.

She didn't really have any definitive ideas on what her discovery could mean, anyway, and she didn't want to come to the wrong conclusion.

But as she'd sorted through the photos she'd taken of the church youth group, she'd noticed something peculiar carved into the trunk of the elm tree the youth had wanted their pictures taken under.

Triple H.

But that was hardly conceivable, was it, that the youths from the church would be responsible for all the mischief that had recently gone down in Wildhorn?

These youths were the best of kids, the teenagers who were always first in line to help whenever it was needed. Were they the young artists who were pranking the neighborhood?

One thing was certain. She wasn't about to share her random, wild theories with Simon, anything that he might latch on to and act upon.

She wasn't even sure she was right. Anyone could have carved that tag into the tree. It didn't have to be the kids in the youth group. The teenagers probably chose the location under the elm tree because it was the prettiest place in the park.

With that, she let it go.

On the day of the adoption event, Miranda

bundled up the twins and headed for Maggie's Pet Store, which was located right next door to Duke's Hardware. All of the shops along the main street were hosting sidewalk sales in conjunction with Simon's event, so there would be plenty of foot traffic and browsing.

Everyone from age zero to one hundred would want to look at the cute doggies—and hopefully some of the onlookers would fall in love with one of the pups and want to take them home to be part of their families.

Miranda had agreed to meet Simon at the pet shop because she already had her hands full with the twins, and he had volunteers coming out to his ranch to help transport the dogs to and from the event.

By the time she got there, Simon had the dogs secured in a dog yard where people could interact with them.

Already in cahoots with Miranda, Maggie Jennings, the pet shop owner, had pasted the oversize poster of Chummy and the twins in the window as a special surprise to Simon—the icing on the cake for what she hoped would be his most successful event ever.

As soon as Simon saw Miranda wheeling the twins toward him, he broke into a big grin. That happened more and more often these days, and Miranda's heart warmed as she grew nearer.

"You continue to surprise me," he said as she approached. "That poster that you made up—"

He swallowed hard and didn't finish his sentence. He didn't have to.

"You're welcome. I'm glad you like it."

"And I'm glad you brought Hudson and Harper with you." He crouched in front of the twins and kissed each of their foreheads. "Of course, you always do, don't you?"

"To be honest, I almost took up my mom's offer to watch them for me today because I'm not sure I'll be much use to you with two wiggly babies to take care of."

"Are you kidding? They are the stars of the show. If the puppies don't draw people in, the babies definitely will."

"You can count on that. Now what else can I do to help?"

"Talk to people? You know that's not my forte."

She laughed. "Ah, yes. But it is mine, isn't it? See how well we complement each other?"

He grinned and tapped the clipboard he was holding. "Send folks my way when the twins have sold them on a puppy. And don't forget to remind them that we deliver Christmas morning. We're as dependable as Santa Claus himself."

"This is so exciting, to think that so many of these precious dogs will go to families who will love them."

She couldn't believe how invested she'd become in Simon's work. She wanted him to succeed, not only for his own sake, but also for the canines he cared so much about. She wanted all the dogs to go to happy homes.

He reached a hand into the dog yard and was immediately surrounded by wet noses and furry ears.

"That's what it's all about," he agreed. "Finding a forever family."

Chapter Fourteen

The adoption event was by far the most success-ful Simon had ever held, which he entirely at-tributed to Miranda and the twins. Among the three of them, they had made all the difference in the world.

It was as easy for Miranda to engage people in meaningful conversation as it was difficult for him. And Harper and Hudson just had to giggle and flap their arms and look cute to get people to cross the street to see what was happening. They'd had a crowded sidewalk all day.

Altogether, they'd received paperwork from fifteen families, and in the week since, Simon had done his due diligence on each of the fami-lies and visited every home to give suggestions and make sure they were dog ready.

He couldn't believe it was Christmas Eve al-ready. Where had the week gone? Time seemed to be rushing by at the speed of light when he wanted to slow down and savor every moment.

Maybe because, for the first time in his life, he felt happy.

Truly happy.

And he was going to attend the Christmas Eve service tonight to thank God for all His blessings. The end of this year marked a complete change in Simon's heart, in more ways than one.

He had a new yet sound and deep-rooted relationship with the Lord, one that he believed gave him hope and a future.

And that future, he prayed, included Miranda and the twins.

He hadn't breathed a word of his faith to anyone yet, because he wanted Miranda to be the first to know how much God was a part of his life now, just as she and the twins were. He knew she'd be thrilled with the news. As with all things, Simon was a private person, and up until today his faith had been between him and God, and the occasional conversation with Mason. He'd given himself time to let it grow and flourish.

Tonight that would all change. He planned to give Miranda the surprise of her life when he waltzed into the sanctuary of the church as if he belonged there—which he did. It was nerve-racking to think about, but faith didn't happen in a vacuum. Mason and Charlotte would also be over the moon with the news. He knew they'd been praying for him for many years, and he would be happy to report that their prayers had been answered.

But even Christmas Eve wouldn't be as exciting as Christmas morning would be. Adrenaline pumped through him as he went over his plans in his head. He'd driven to another town earlier this week to purchase an engagement ring, knowing if he'd gone into the local jewelry store, the news would be all over town by the end of the day.

He'd kept the secret—and the ring—close to his heart, both literally and figuratively, in all the days following. Right in his shirt pocket. He might not be as creative as Miranda, but after much thought, he believed he'd put together a proposal she would never forget.

His affection for her had grown over the month and a half they'd been together. He'd only had to get out of his own way and be willing to put a label on it.

He was in love with Miranda.

He hoped and prayed she returned the sentiment. He would know for sure tomorrow morning. It would either be the best Christmas present ever or the worst holiday of his life. One or the other, and there was only one way to find out.

It was early in the day yet, but he kept checking his phone and glancing out the front window, anxious for Miranda to arrive at the ranch with the twins. They were coming over to help give all of the dogs a bath, and then the fortunate adoptees would be corralled out in the kennels until it was time to make Christmas morning deliveries.

He laughed when he thought of the twins helping with the baths. He remembered how wet his jeans had gotten with Harper in the tub. She might even be more enthusiastic as a "helper." He'd stocked up on extra towels, knowing his entire bathroom—and probably everyone in it— was bound to get soaked.

His heart warmed until he thought it might burst. How could a man possibly be as happy as he was right now?

After tomorrow he would have a real forever family to care for and love, for as long as he lived. He would no longer be alone. And he planned to count his blessings every second of every day from now until forever.

Miranda honked as she pulled up in front of his place. He missed the high, piercing sound of her convertible, but he didn't think she ever thought about it at all. She'd adapted everything in her life to make room for the twins.

He counted to ten and then burst through the door and strode out to meet them. He didn't want to seem too eager, but he expected his expression was a dead giveaway.

Could he blame his joy on the holiday and the success of his adoption event, or would Miranda see right through him?

"I thought we'd better start with the adoptees," Simon said as he unhooked Hudson from his car seat. "If we don't get to the other dogs, it's no big deal. We can always wash them later. But I want the ones going to their forever families to look their very best."

"This is exciting," Miranda said enthusiastically as she took the helm of the bathtub, the sprayer in her hand. "I'm so happy for every one of these dogs."

"It's a good day for everyone," Simon agreed, handing her the first pup on the list. Miranda used the sprayer to wet the dogs and, with the twins' "helping" by splashing water all over the bathroom, soaped them up and hosed them down. Simon stood behind them with towels at the ready.

As he'd suspected, the water didn't exactly stay in the tub. Some of the dogs, like the labs, loved the water and didn't object at all to being bathed. Others, like the Chihuahua, not so much. Taco looked like a miserable drowned rat when Miranda and the twins got through with him. But he was going to a wonderful forever home with a senior couple who had instantly fallen in love with him at the adoption event.

After the fifteen dogs were washed and kenneled, Simon brought Zig and Zag in for a bath.

Miranda's face fell. "They've been adopted?"

Simon nodded.

"Oh. I guess I was so busy I didn't see them at the adoption event."

"They weren't there. This is a private adoption. The family has a couple of kids who I think will really love the Westies."

She tried to smile, but it didn't quite reach her eyes. "I'm sure they will. The twins certainly like them. They'll be missed."

"Mmm."

He turned away from her. He just couldn't look her in the eyes right now. Her expression nearly broke his heart.

When Zig and Zag were bathed and were zipping through the house chasing each other in their usual method of blow-drying their fur, Simon pulled on his jean jacket. "I'm going to go feed the dogs and spend a few minutes with the ones leaving tomorrow. Do you want to come with me?"

"Very much. Just help me get the twins bundled up."

It took a few minutes to get the babies into their coats. Miranda was quicker than Simon and somehow managed to get Hudson's arms where they needed to go. Harper apparently didn't feel like wearing her jacket, because every time he got close to putting her arm in the appropriate sleeve, she'd pull away.

"Be a good girl for Uncle Simon and put your army through your sleevey," Miranda said, taking Harper into her arms. "You're just creating trouble so you'll get more attention, aren't you, little miss?"

Simon met Miranda's gaze and smiled.

"Remember that first day, when I told you I had concerns about you becoming Hudson and Harper's guardian?" he asked.

"It's hard to forget. You were pretty forthright with me."

"Rude, you mean."

"Your words, not mine." She laughed.

"I was also wrong. Very wrong. You are a wonderful mother to the twins. It's been a blessing for me to watch you bond with them, and they with you. Mary's and John's deaths were a terrible tragedy, but they made the right choice in giving Hudson and Harper into your care. There's no doubt in my mind that you three were meant to be together."

Four, perhaps?

Her eyes brightened. "Do you really think so? I still have moments when I wonder if I'm doing enough for them."

"You love them with your whole heart, and

they love you right back again. The rest of it is just icing on the cake."

"Thank you."

She ran a hand down his arm and every nerve ending came alive as she squeezed his hand. When their eyes met, it was all he could do not to steal a kiss, despite the twins perched between them.

He didn't want to give himself away, but she was just too beautiful to resist. He leaned in, intending to brush his lips across her cheek, but her gaze widened and she moved away before he could make contact.

His pulse jolted in surprise.

Did she not want him to kiss her?

If that was the case, this was going to be the worst weekend of his life.

"It's going to be dark soon," she said, fussing with Hudson's jacket. "We'd best get out and see your doggies."

He took Harper back into his arms and followed Miranda out the door, his mind rehashing every moment since the time they'd kissed right in the middle of Tumbleweed Avenue. He hadn't attempted to kiss her again until now, but she hadn't given him any reason to think she wouldn't welcome his affection.

What if he was all wrong about this?

What if she didn't return his regard?

He continued behind her toward the kennels, his head lowered in thought and his gaze on the ground.

He'd been alone most of his life, but until now, he'd never been lonely. Not until now. Miranda and the twins had filled his heart in a way he never could have imagined.

"Simon?"

Miranda came to a dead stop and Simon's boots skidded in the dirt to keep from running into her.

The sound of her voice—

Surprise.

A note of panic.

He looked up, his gaze following the direction of hers.

"Did I misunderstand you? Are the dogs in the barn and not the kennels?"

His heart fell into his gut, which was turning like a combine.

Oh, Lord, please. Anything but this.

The kennels were empty, and the gate to his property was swinging in the wind.

His dogs had vanished.

"You put the dogs into the kennels, right?" She was trying to keep the alarm she was feeling out of her tone but she knew she was failing miserably. Her heart was pounding wildly in her chest and her breath was coming in short bursts.

How could this have happened?

Simon's mouth opened and closed but no words came out. Miranda watched his face blanch under his stubble.

"Where are they?" he ground out coarsely. "Where are my dogs? I know I shut the kennel doors. And the gate—"

From a distance came the sound of barking. At first it was just one or two dogs, but then the chorus picked up and howling filled the entire neighborhood.

Simon scrambled for the barn. The door was open there, as well. Dash was still stabled, but the cattle dogs were missing.

All of them. Even the puppies.

"Someone's been in here. They stole the dogs. What am I going to do, Miranda?" His voice was coming in sharp, staccato bursts, his tone somewhere between panic and tears. "My whole life's work. They're all gone. If I lose the dogs, I've lost everything. I've got to go after them."

She reached for his hand to steady him.

"Before we go off half-cocked, let's go back inside and think things through."

"There's no time for that." Simon's voice had risen an octave.

"It's better if we stop and make a plan," she

said, taking his hand and urging him to return to the house. She placed the twins in a portable playpen so they couldn't get into too much mischief and turned her attention fully on Simon. "There's two of us. If we split up, we can cover more ground, as long as we're not crossing over each other. And I'm not positive the dogs have been stolen. With the cacophony out there, it sounds like your dogs are all over the neighborhood. I think they got out on their own somehow and escaped through the gate."

He groaned. "That's even worse. I don't know how that could have happened. I know I shut the kennels tight, and the gate was closed when I came back inside the house.

"If they're running all over town, I'll never get them all back. Think of all the kids who won't get their puppy on Christmas morning. And my herding dogs—I can't replace them. And even if I could, I was training a few ranchers' dogs for them. What am I going to tell them? That I lost their expensive cattle dogs?" He sank onto the couch and put his head in his hands. "I'm done for. Finished."

"I don't believe that." She had no idea how she was going to fix this problem, but Simon was *not* going to lose his life's work in one fell swoop. She would do anything in her power to see that didn't happen.

She had to figure this out, and fast.

"The kennels were open. The barn door was open. And so was the gate. If it wasn't someone trying to steal your dogs, then—"

"It was the pranksters," Simon finished for her. "I told you things were going to get out of hand. I just didn't realize I'd be the victim."

His words could have been an accusation, but they weren't. They were more of a statement of fact, as if he had already given up.

"Simon, listen to me. The pranksters. I think I know who they are."

His head snapped up. "You *what*?"

Now she had his full attention. His eyes blazed into hers.

"What do you mean you know who they are? You're part of the neighborhood watch team. You were supposed to report them to me if you caught them in action."

"Well, that's just it. I didn't exactly catch them in action. I—"

She paused. "It will be easier for me to show you than to tell you. Can you watch the twins for a moment while I go get my camera?"

He nodded, his expression stony. Harper and Hudson were contentedly playing in the pop-up playpen Simon had bought for use at his house.

He was going to blame her for this—and maybe he'd be right in doing so. She *was* a member of the neighborhood watch. She should have told Simon about her theory as soon as she'd discovered it herself.

But she'd stayed silent, and now, because she hadn't spoken up when she first found out, Simon might be losing everything that was dear to him.

She couldn't imagine why the church youth group teens would play a cruel prank like this. They had to know how important Simon's dogs were to him, even if he wasn't a member of the church.

Simon was right. The pranks had gone from innocent to harmful.

But one piece of the puzzle didn't fit.

There was nothing artistic about letting dogs loose.

She stopped just short of Simon's porch and looked around for clues. What had the teenagers meant by this cruel act? Was it possible it was even the same people, or was it someone who'd taken advantage of the teenagers' mischief to do something harmful that they'd be blamed for?

"Hold on a moment," she said, racing outside to get her camera from the car. As she approached the porch, she took a determined look around. Her heart fell when she saw the evergreen wreath Simon had hung on his door. Inside, someone had placed a carved wooden Triple H.

So it was the youth group.

"I'm so sorry," she said as she reentered the ranch house. "This is all my fault. I knew who it was, and I didn't say anything."

"How *could* you?"

She understood why he was directing his anger at her, and she didn't blame him for it in the least.

She pulled up the photos on her camera and found the ones she'd taken of the youth group under the elm tree in the park.

"What am I looking for?" Simon asked. "Is this the bunch of kids who just ruined my life?"

"This is the church youth group," she admitted miserably.

"The church youth group?" he parroted. "I don't believe it."

"Neither did I. That's why I didn't say anything. But if you look at the trunk of the tree just above where the teenagers are standing, you'll see a carving of the Triple H brand."

"How long have you known? Why didn't you tell me?"

"Because I thought it must be a mistake. I rationalized my way out of my original conclusions. I figured that anyone could have put that mark there. It didn't have to be the youth group."

"Which is true."

"Yes, except they specifically asked me to photograph them under that tree. I think it might have been a joke to them."

"I'm not laughing."

"Neither am I," she agreed gravely.

"What now?" He shoved both hands into his hair. "We both go and canvass the neighborhoods looking for the dogs? Even if I find some of them, I don't see how I can recover from this."

"Not if it's just the two of us. Let me make a phone call. We need all the help we can get."

She went into the kitchen to call Pastor Corbit. She had an idea, but she wasn't sure Simon would go along with it. She thought it was better that she just put the plan in motion and then tell him what it was.

She returned to the living room a minute later.

"The youth group is on its way over. We'll mobilize them to canvass the neighborhoods in cars and on foot. And Pastor Corbit has contacted the prayer chain. Everyone in town will know to look out for your dogs."

"You're bringing the *pranksters* over here to look for my dogs?" he asked, astounded. "Why would you do that?"

"Because despite everything, I think they want to help. There are some things that still don't add up. There is nothing remotely artistic about what they've done today. I want to hear their explanation before I call in a judgment."

"I'm not as kind as you. I want to call the police, except that I'd end up with animal control coming out and I'll be the one taking the brunt of all this. Fat lot of good building the privacy fence along the south border did me."

"You already are." She brushed her palm across his face but he jerked away from her, refusing to meet her gaze.

"Let me talk to the youths. I think I hear some of them approaching now." She was afraid he might lose his temper with the kids before she was able to find out what had actually occurred. Somehow, she felt like there was more to the story than a group of teenagers sneaking onto a ranch in the dark and freeing all the dogs from Simon's rescue so they would run off into the night.

That just didn't sound right.

It wasn't long before the entire group was assembled out in Simon's front yard. She could tell by the looks on their faces that they were as appalled by what happened as she felt.

"Who wants to tell me what's going on?" she asked gravely.

They all looked at each other without speaking. After a few seconds a boy with his hair dyed as black as night stepped forward. Miranda recognized him as Owen Blake, the son of a local rancher.

"It's my fault. We all let the dogs out of their kennels, but I was the last one out. We heard a noise and thought someone was coming, so we left in a hurry. I must not have closed the gate correctly. I didn't mean for this to happen, Miss Morgan, but I'm the one to blame. The rest of the group isn't at fault."

Another boy stepped forward. "I opened the barn door. I got sidetracked by the puppies. I must not have shut the door behind me when I left. You can blame me, too."

"Let's not point fingers here. We're running out of time. Do you want to tell me why you all were here sneaking around in the first place?"

"The dog adoptions," a girl with a short blond bob said. Her name was Wendy, although Miranda couldn't remember whose daughter she was. "We brought out Christmas ribbons to put bows around their necks, since they'll all be presents for little kids. We let the dogs wander outside the kennels because we thought Mr. West would be sure and notice them that way. We had some extra ribbon left over, and we thought it might be a nice surprise for Mr. West if we put bows on his cattle dog puppies."

"That's lovely," Miranda said. "I knew in my heart you all were trying to do something nice."

"Yeah, but I messed it all up," Owen said miserably. "Now all of Mr. West's dogs are gone."

"We've already got the prayer chain going to let folks around town know to look out for stray dogs. We're asking ranchers to saddle up and check out their acreages. How many of you have cars?"

Several of the teenagers raised their hands.

"Go in small groups. Park at the end of a street and canvass the neighborhoods by foot. Let's designate a couple of you to bring Simon's dogs back to the ranch as you find them. Who has a truck?"

Nearly everyone who'd initially raised their hands when Miranda had asked about having a vehicle raised their hands again. This was the country, and most of the residents of Wildhorn were ranchers. Folks tended to own trucks over cars so they could tow horse trailers.

They quickly organized who was going where, and who would be bringing the dogs back to the ranch. Miranda was staying at the ranch and playing point person. Everyone put her cell number on their phone before they left.

After a few final instructions, she walked everyone out past the gate and waved as they took off down the lane, then decided to check the barn.

As she entered, she thought she heard a sound from the far end of the barn. It was already twilight and it was getting more and more difficult to see by the minute. Soon it would be full-on night. Miranda prayed most of the dogs would be found before then. She didn't want to think about what would happen to the ones who got away.

She pulled the gate of the farthest stall open,

looking for the source of the sounds, and was delighted to see five little roly-poly puppies in a box half-covered in Christmas wrap with a roll of tape nearby. Someone had clearly moved them from the stall nearest the entrance, but it was equally obvious that that person had left in a hurry, just as the other teens had done. The puppies were all bedecked in red and green bows, crawling over each other as their mama paced around the box.

"Shadow," Miranda said, crouching to pet the blue heeler's neck. "Boy, am I glad to see you. And all of your puppies, of course. Let's get you back to the stall where you belong, so I can bring Simon some good news."

Chapter Fifteen

Just when Simon thought it couldn't get worse, it got worse.

He was sitting on the sofa, watching the twins play and waiting for Miranda to come back inside and tell him why the youth group had ruined his life. He expected she'd probably have some kind of fancy story to tell, giving him some reason she thought he ought to forgive them for what they'd done.

Was this how Jesus felt in the Garden of Gethsemane, when His friends had turned their backs on Him and He had lost everything?

He had no idea what he was going to do next. He supposed that partially depended on how many dogs they managed to round up, and how many would be lost to him permanently. It made him sick to his stomach just to think about it.

What was he going to tell all those excited children on Christmas morning, when they woke up and didn't find their puppy underneath the tree?

And what about the ranchers whose investments in their cattle dogs had now disappeared under his watch? He didn't have the money to pay them back for what they'd lost, although he'd find the way to do it somehow, even if it took him years.

Chummy bumped Simon's hand with his wet nose, demanding affection, but Simon barely noticed. Chummy jumped onto the couch and burrowed in his lap, determined to make him feel better.

He sighed. At least he hadn't lost Chummy. And Loki was lying down by the fire. Zig and Zag were around somewhere, although now all of his plans with those two had been completely dashed to pieces on the rocks. With his life in ruins, he could not possibly ask Miranda and Hudson and Harper to be a part of it.

He'd lost his reputation.

He'd lost his dogs.

And now he was going to lose Miranda and the twins.

He didn't even know how to start over, but whatever he did, he wasn't going to drag Miranda down with him. She was loyal to a fault, and he knew she wouldn't abandon him in his time of need. But she would never know about his true feelings for her, because he was never going to share them with her.

She deserved better, and though it would shatter his heart into billions of pieces to let her go, he knew that was what he had to do. It was the *right* thing to do. He couldn't tell her how he felt now.

His cell phone chirped and jerked him out of his thoughts, startling him so much that he almost dropped it.

Good news?

Had someone found one of his dogs?

"Hello?" he said tentatively.

"How dare you let one of your dogs loose to roam about in the streets in the middle of the night."

Blanche Stanton. Exaggerating as usual.

"You've seen one of my dogs?"

"I have it right here. I found it wandering around in my bushes. A little gray fluffy thing. It doesn't bite, does it?"

"That's Sasha, my senior toy poodle mix, and no, *she* doesn't bite. She's one of the sweetest dogs I have."

How had Sasha gotten out? She wasn't even outside with the rest of them. She must have slipped off when he'd been distracted.

"Well, I don't appreciate her nosing around my house."

"Look, Blanche, it's been kind of a rough day.

I'll come get her as soon as I'm able, okay? But it might be a little while."

"Don't bother," Blanche said gruffly. "I'm bringing her back to you. And I'm going to stay right there at your ranch until the animal control officer arrives. I've already called in to report you. Do you hear me?"

Simon didn't answer. His breath had been punched from his lungs.

He was in trouble. Big trouble.

Even if they found most of the dogs, he'd still be accountable for having let them escape, as well he should be. At the end of the day, he was responsible for every one of his dogs. And if they got into any mischief, it was all on him.

None of his dogs was unfriendly. They'd all passed the AKC Good Citizen's certification. But he knew some people considered dogs in general dangerous. Officer Peterson had given him a break last time he'd visited, but there would be no bending rules this time, especially with Blanche Stanton looking on.

"Guess who I found," Miranda said as she came inside the house.

He was leaning on his elbows, staring at the floor, and he didn't even bother to look up. He couldn't stand to look Miranda in the eyes right now.

Not because he was angry with her. He didn't

know why she had kept her suspicions about the youth group a secret, but he was sure she had her reasons. The truth was, he didn't want to let her see him with tears in his eyes, in his greatest moment of weakness.

He was heartbroken.

"I found Shadow and her babies in one of the stalls in the barn," Miranda continued animatedly, but Simon couldn't wrap his mind around her words. "One of the teens must have moved them to the back of the barn, but they're safe and sound. All five puppies. I made sure the door was shut good and tight this time."

Shadow was safe. That was good news. And her puppies. Could he make a new start with one dog and her puppies?

"Simon, did you hear me? I found Shadow and the puppies. Isn't that good news?"

When he didn't respond, she sank down next to him on the couch and put her arm around his shoulders.

"This isn't over yet. We're working on getting all the dogs corralled as we speak. I've got the entire youth group out looking for them, and the church prayer chain is spreading the word throughout town to be on the lookout for stray dogs. It hasn't been that long. They can't have gone far. We'll get them all back, Simon. I know we will."

He held his cell phone up for her inspection.

"One dog has already been found. I just got off the phone."

"What? Well, that's good news, too, right?"

He shook his head.

"No. It's not. It's my toy poodle mix, Sasha. She wasn't with the adoptees. She must have skipped out when I was preoccupied and frantic about the other ones. The poor little thing is a senior, so the chances of adopting her out were always slim. But now…"

He groaned and scrubbed a hand through his hair.

"She must be scared to death," he finished, thinking of the poor dog cowering under Blanche's typically sour mood.

"But you said someone found her?"

He lifted his head and groaned again.

"I just got off the phone with Blanche Stanton. Apparently, she found Sasha wandering around in her bushes."

"Oh, no."

"Oh, no is right. I told her I'd come get Sasha when I had a moment, but she's on her way over with the dog as we speak."

"Well, that is nice of her—I guess."

"Not so much. She called Officer Peterson and reported me, and she intends to stay at the ranch until the officer does his duty and shuts me down for good. Hopefully it's not an arrestable offense. I don't really want to be dragged off in handcuffs tonight."

He was kidding, trying to lighten the mood a little bit, but Miranda turned as white as a sheet.

"I'm joking. About being carried off in handcuffs. Not about Blanche Stanton and Officer Peterson being on their way."

Miranda's phone rang and she held up a finger as she listened to whatever the person on the other end of the line was saying.

"One of the groups is heading in with the first load of dogs. Four of your cattle dogs. So we only have one more cattle dog to go, right? You have four females and two males, counting Shadow?"

He nodded. At least Shadow was the only one who had puppies at present. "And four that belong to other ranchers."

"We'll have to keep looking, then. The group coming in says they also have a handful of other dogs," she continued. "I've had text messages from all around town. Your adoptees are being found and picked up one after the other, Simon. Everybody is out looking for them. It's going to be okay."

For one short moment, he brightened. It was so

easy to get caught up in what Miranda was saying that he almost believed everything *would* be okay.

But then he remembered Blanche and Officer Peterson.

Even if the dogs were all on their way back, which was unlikely, he still had to deal with the consequences. This wasn't going to go away just because he wanted it to. The entire town knew his dogs had gotten loose. Officer Peterson surely would have heard that it was more than just Sasha. And members of the youth group would be in and out of his ranch house all evening, delivering his dogs back to him—he hoped.

How would he explain *that* to the officer?

"I have an idea," Miranda said as if reading his mind. "I think I know how to work this out so that Officer Peterson has other things to think about than where your dogs are, or why you've got the youth group swarming around your house. But I'm going to need your help, and we're going to have to work quickly."

She paused dramatically. "We're going to throw a Christmas party."

Miranda wasn't sure how this was going to work out in practice, but in theory, everything looked great. They'd had to improvise, since Simon didn't have many Christmas decorations. She'd sent him outside to collect any greenery that looked even remotely Christmas-like. She hoped he would also get a good breath of fresh air while he was at it.

Owen had shown up with what was left of the ribbon they'd used on the dogs, and he and his small group set right to work making the living room look festive. She found an old disco light in Simon's linen closet—she'd have to ask him about that sometime—and she cut out and hung up a fake mistletoe sprig made from colored copy paper in the doorway between the living room and kitchen.

It wasn't perfect, but hopefully it would be enough.

She'd called each small group and let them in on the plan. After they had canvassed their assigned neighborhood, they were to return to Simon's ranch for the party. Afterward, they'd all attend the midnight church service together.

Amazingly, at last count there were only two dogs missing—one cattle dog and one rescue. Miranda held out hope that both of the final two would be found.

She lowered the lamps and turned on the disco light to red and green, which threw soft outlines across the ceiling and walls. She'd just plugged in her cell phone to Simon's surround sound so she could stream Christmas music when someone banged on the front door.

It didn't sound like teenagers. Miranda held up a hand to Simon to let him know she'd answer it.

Blanche stood on the doorstep, Sasha cradled in one arm. Her expression was somewhere between annoyed and exasperated.

"Do you know how hard it is to drive with a puppy on your lap?" she asked, pushing past Miranda and into the house. "Are you having a party in here?"

"Yes, and you're welcome to join us. I can take Sasha. She's a senior, you know, and not a puppy."

"She is?" Blanche glanced down at Sasha, but made no move to pass her into Miranda's outstretched hand. "Well, isn't that interesting?"

Miranda dropped her arm. If she wasn't mistaken, Blanche had drawn Sasha nearer to her. She'd thought the toy poodle would be afraid of Blanche, but they seemed to be getting on very well.

"Why don't you come on over and make yourself at home in this armchair?" she suggested, gesturing to the most comfortable chair in the room.

For the first time Miranda was seeing Blanche as a different person—a tired, lonely old lady in need of company. Once she'd been seated by the fire, she looked rather content watching the teenagers mingling, with Sasha curled up and sleeping on her lap.

Maybe she'd misjudged Blanche.

Time would tell.

She looked for the opportunity to pull Simon aside, but two new groups of teenagers arrived with bottles of punch and packages of Christmas cookies.

"Great idea, guys," she told them.

She peeked outside. The dogs slated to go to adoptive homes the next day were all back in the kennels, still wearing their festive bows. A few of them were a little worse for the wear from their nighttime jaunt, but nothing a washcloth and a little soap couldn't fix. They could deal with that in the morning.

Her phone buzzed. A rancher had found one of Simon's cattle dogs practicing on his herd. Miranda texted back that she'd send one of the teenagers out immediately to pick up the blue heeler and bring him back to the ranch.

Miranda wanted to pump her fist. One down, and only one to go.

No—wait.

Blanche had brought in Sasha, and Miranda had forgotten to count the toy poodle.

Unbelievable. Every dog present and accounted for. She couldn't wait to share the good news with Simon.

She found him leaning his shoulder against the doorway between the living room and the kitchen, his arms crossed over his chest and a despondent expression on his face as he watched the teenagers interact. The twins were wide-awake, and some of the members of the youth group had taken them from the playpen and were sitting on the floor with Hudson and Harper in their laps.

Any misapprehension she'd felt earlier when Simon had tried to kiss her dissipated. Up until tonight, she'd still questioned her ability to trust herself and her choices.

Miranda was done second-guessing herself—and Simon. She stepped in beside Simon and slid her arm around his waist, filling up the door frame. When he glanced down at her, she smiled, but he didn't return the grin, nor did he put his arm around her as she'd hoped he'd do. Apparently, he hadn't noticed the mistletoe hanging above them—or maybe she'd done such a poor job creating it that he couldn't even tell it *was* mistletoe.

Bad or good, no matter what, they were together. If they could work through this, they could work through anything.

But this latest news?

This was beyond great. It was fantastic. God was good.

"I've been tallying up the dogs that have come back in. We have five of your cattle dogs back in the barn, as well as the four you were holding in training. A rancher just found number six out herding his cattle for him. I sent one of the teens for him."

She felt the breath leave his chest.

"That's good. Great. But we'll have to wait and see what Officer Peterson has to say about what happened tonight. I'm responsible for that. Despite all the work I've done on the south fence, he still may take the dogs away. I wouldn't blame him, really. I can't have my dogs running around the neighborhood unsupervised. And there are still going to be disappointed children tomorrow morning if we don't capture all the rescues."

"There's absolutely no reason for Kyle to go to any trouble whatsoever. As soon as he gets here, I'll send him on his way. I came over to tell you that *all* of the adoptees are back in the kennels. Most of them still even look like they've been bathed recently, if you can believe it. You're still going to get to be every bit as dependable as Santa Claus," she said, remembering what he'd once told her.

Simon slid down the door frame until he was seated, clutching his knees to his chest and breathing heavily.

"Thank God. Thank God. Thank God."

She crouched next to him, her heart warming and swelling in her chest. She loved this man so much. The intensity of her feelings surprised her.

"Thank God, indeed."

"Where is Blanche? I saw her come in earlier."

"She's sitting in the armchair by the fire."

"Do you think she's going to give us any trouble? I'm already in enough as it is."

Miranda smiled softly. "I think you should go look for yourself."

Simon's eyes widened, but he stood and walked over to the armchair. Miranda watched as he bent over the woman. She was surprised at how long they spoke. Usually their conversations were short and abrupt.

He was shaking his head when he returned to Miranda's side.

"What's the verdict?" she asked.

"Turns out we're going to have sixteen adoptees ready to go home to their forever families. It appears that Blanche now has a new best friend."

"Sasha?"

He chuckled. "Who would have guessed it, huh? Blanche being a dog person? Maybe we misjudged her."

"I think you're right. She's just a lonely old lady. And the teenagers? They didn't mean to let your dogs out. They were trying to put Christmas ribbons on all of them when they were spooked by a noise. I hope you can find it in your heart to forgive them."

"I'm still trying to wrap my mind around getting all my dogs back. They really jumped to it. Maybe the teens really were trying to spread Christmas cheer. Which means the other pranks were probably made in good fun, as well. I wouldn't have given them the chance to make things right."

"Exactly. It's not easy to forgive."

He narrowed his eyes on her, taking in her measure.

"Why do I feel like we're not talking about the youth group here?"

"Do you know why I left Wildhorn?" she countered.

"To become a celebrity photographer," he answered promptly, looking at her as if she was one cookie short of a dozen.

"To get away from you."

"What?"

"I know, right? You probably didn't give me a second thought, did you? And yet I ran away from Wildhorn to get away from you."

"I have no idea what you're talking about."

"You aren't the only one who's ever been the butt end of a mean, hateful joke. I've never been thrown in a Dumpster, but that doesn't mean that I wasn't affected by jokes—mean pranks."

"I hate to admit it, but all I vaguely remember about you is that you were my best friend's kid sister. It wasn't until much later that I…well… continue with your story."

"You don't remember setting me up, leading me to believe that you had asked me to your senior prom? That you and Mason wrote a note to me asking me to be your date?"

She took a deep breath. Even though she knew in her heart that Simon was a different man now, it was still hard to talk about her impressionable past.

"I was so excited that you'd finally noticed me, and I was just foolish enough not to confirm that date directly with you. Maybe if I had, you wouldn't have gone through with it."

"Oh, boy," he said, shoving his hand into his hair. "I think I see where this is going, and it isn't good."

"Right. I spent all of my savings on the prettiest dress I could afford. I got my hair done at a salon, and even splurged on my very first manipedi. I wanted to look absolutely perfect for you."

"I was such a jerk." His gaze flooded with sympathy.

"Of course, I wanted to make a grand entrance. I wanted you to look at me and see only me, just like in the movies. I waited at the top of the stairs for an hour until I heard you arrive. And then—"

"Then you saw me walk in with my real date to the prom."

"Yes. I was halfway down the stairs before I realized you and Mason had set me up. I'd never been more mortified in my life. As I was running up the stairs in distress, you and Mason broke out into loud laughter that cut me to the quick. By that point, I'd been crushing on you for two years, you know."

"You were? You did?" His mouth kicked up into a heart-stopping half smile.

"Don't look so smug." She swatted at his arm.

"That was seriously the reason you left town? Because of me? You had two years of high school left. Surely you moved on from one stupid prank."

"You still came to my house to hang out with Mason. I couldn't avoid you, and it took me a long time to put the incident in my past."

"But you aren't like me. You don't hold grudges."

"It's a learned art, one that I mastered over time, because I realized that keeping those feelings close was hurting me, not you."

"Did you ever confront Mason about this?"

"Eventually. It was easier to forgive my brother than the boy who broke my heart."

"Wow. Just—wow. I am so, so sorry."

"Don't be. I'm over it. But I hope you won't be too hard on the teenagers. They really meant well, no matter how it looked to us earlier. There was no malice intended."

He cringed. "Not like me, you mean."

She squeezed his hand. "I forgive you. I forgave you long ago."

She would have said more, but at that moment someone knocked on the door. The teenagers had just been letting themselves in without knocking, and the final cattle dog had been reported as returned to the barn—with the door double-checked as tightly closed—so Miranda had a pretty good notion of who was pounding so firmly.

She started toward the door but Simon stopped her.

"I've got this one."

He let Officer Peterson in and shook hands with him.

"I've been expecting you."

"Oddly, I had a number of encounters on my way to your ranch. I had the distinct impression your neighbors were trying to slow me down."

Miranda tensed, holding her breath and praying for Simon.

"They were," Simon confirmed. "They were trying to give me time to get my dogs back after they got loose. I'm sure you've heard. It was pretty much chaos tonight."

Miranda was surprised that Simon was so open and honest about what had happened, but she supposed she shouldn't have been. He'd always been the type of man to own up to what he considered his mistakes.

"And did you?" Kyle asked. "Get all of your dogs back?"

"I did. Would you believe, with the youth group's help, that we found every last one of them?"

"I'm happy to hear that. I know you've worked hard to build up your business and the rescue shelter. How did they get out, anyway?"

Miranda's gaze shifted back to Simon. She didn't know what he was going to say, but she trusted him enough to know he wouldn't purposefully get the teenagers in trouble.

He merely shrugged. "The gate got left open."

That was all he said. Not how. Not who. Just that it had been left open. And that was the truth.

"Well, all's well that ends well, I guess. Except I haven't yet spoken to—"

"Officer Peterson." Blanche stepped forward, Sasha tucked up against her chest. "I'm the one that called in with the complaint."

He nodded and pulled out his pad to take notes.

"I know, Mrs. Stanton. Please go ahead with your complaint. I'm sorry, Simon, but I do have to formally report this," the officer said.

"No worries," Simon responded.

"Put that notepad away," Blanche barked, waving her free hand at the officer. "I'm rescinding my complaint."

Officer Peterson's eyes grew large.

"You are? But—"

"But nothing, young man. Now, can't you see we're having a party here?"

"And you're welcome to join us, Kyle," Miranda said, stepping into the fray. She couldn't hide her smile at the way Blanche had turned everything around as easily as she'd stirred things up. "Although we'll soon be leaving for church for the midnight service."

"I'll be there. But I'd rather change into a suit. So if you'll excuse me, I'll be on my way."

As the officer walked away, Simon swept Miranda into his arms and hugged her so hard her feet left the floor.

"You are amazing," he whispered into her ear. "I thought my world had ended tonight. How did you do this?"

"With a lot of help from our friends," she said, gesturing around the room at the kids gathered in social circles.

"Oh, stop it, you two," Blanche said feistily. "You'll set a bad example for the teenagers."

"Speaking of which," Miranda said, "it's time for me to gather them all up and get to church. I don't like leaving your house such a mess, though. I promise I'll come over tomorrow and clean it all up."

"No, you absolutely will not. It's Christmas morning. You are going to spend Christmas at home with the twins."

"We're celebrating at Mason and Charlotte's house. I'm sure they wouldn't mind if you came, as well. There's bound to be plenty of food," she said hopefully.

"I would, but I'm afraid I have plans of my own."

"Oh." She hadn't expected that answer, and she didn't know how to respond, so she turned to the teenagers and flickered the lights to get their attention.

"It's time for us to go to the midnight service," she announced. "But before you leave, I would just like to thank you for all your help tonight. Thanks to you, we got every dog back where they belong."

The teenagers clapped and hooted.

"That said, I would like to organize one more service project. I think you'll all agree that today was pretty chaotic."

There were many nods and murmurs.

"So, to make up for it, tomorrow morning, you all are going to gather in the same groups as you did this evening and make some special deliveries. Since you like being sneaky so much—now you're going to do it for a good cause."

The teenagers cheered and started gathering their coats.

The youths who were holding Hudson and Harper handed them to Miranda and Simon, and everyone dispersed.

Owen approached, looking ashamed of himself.

"I just want to say again how sorry I am," he said to Simon. "I was the last one out of the gate, and I should have double-checked that it was closed properly. I would have felt really bad if you hadn't gotten all your dogs back."

Simon clapped the youth on the shoulder. "But we did. It's forgiven and forgotten, son. Now get yourself to church."

"I do have one more question," Miranda said before the black-haired young man turned away. "Owen, what's with the tag?"

"Tag?" he asked, his confused gaze sweeping from Miranda to Simon and back again.

Miranda's gaze met Simon's and they both burst into laughter.

Simon had been thinking the pranks might be gang activity, and Owen, who appeared to be one of the youth group leaders, didn't even know what a *tag* was.

"The brand," she clarified. "Triple H."

Owen grinned. "I'm surprised more people haven't figured it out by now, seeing as it's Christmas and all."

He paused and bobbed his dark eyebrows. "*Ho, Ho, Ho.* Triple H."

Miranda laughed so hard she snorted.

"Clever," Simon said, having a difficult time controlling his own laughter. "Miranda's right. Y'all *are* very artistic."

"Thank you, sir."

"Now, get on your way. We've got to get the twins bundled up. It's time for us to head for church."

Miranda turned to Simon, her mouth agape.

"Us?"

"Do you have a problem with that?" he asked, grinning.

"No, of course not. It's just surprising, is all."

He kissed her cheek.

"Isn't that what Christmas is all about? Surprises?"

She pressed a hand to her cheek where he'd kissed her and nodded.

"Then Merry Christmas, darlin'."

Chapter Sixteen

After the chaos and confusion of yesterday evening, Simon was glad he'd still been able to surprise Miranda by accompanying her to church. Her look of sheer delight was worth every time he had to bite his tongue not to give away his secret earlier.

Mason and Charlotte were pretty stoked to see him darken the door of the church, as well. They introduced him to everyone he didn't know and many whom he did, they were so happy he was with them.

If he'd surprised Miranda, she wasn't half as astonished as he'd been by his first real church experience—how welcomed he felt by the parishioners, and most especially how wonderful it was to worship God with them and sing Christmas hymns loud and strong, if a little off-key. He was sorry he'd missed out all these years, but now he'd come home.

Speaking of home, he had a lot to do this morning. He had *tagged*—laughing at his own pun as he did it—each of the adopted dogs, and the teenagers had arrived to make their special deliveries. He enjoyed watching the excitement in their eyes at the prospect and realized some of them might appreciate volunteering for the shelter.

He'd always been a one-man band, depending only on himself to do all the work, but now he was beginning to realize that being all alone wasn't necessarily best. He couldn't imagine his life without Miranda and the twins. And now he'd have extra help from the teenagers who'd agreed to assist him in grooming and training the rescue dogs. The kids would be doing something both useful and fun, and that felt good, too.

After making sure all of the dogs got where they were supposed to go, with each teenager checking in by text when their present was delivered, he showered and dressed in jeans and his newest red chambray shirt. He wanted to look his very best today, so he'd picked a festive color that went along with the Christmas season, knowing Miranda would appreciate it even if this was all new territory for him. He'd never before in his life thought about what he was wearing. Any shirt and jeans would do.

But not today.

That was what having a wonderful woman in his life did to a man. She made him a better person, inside and out.

Complicated? Yes. But worth every crazy moment.

Combing his hair in the mirror, he rehearsed what he was going to say. He'd actually taken the time to write his speech down and memorize it. He intended to do this only once, and he didn't want to mess it up.

That was going to be the hardest part of the day—speaking his heart. But this day wasn't very well going to go the way he wanted it to if he couldn't get the words out of his mouth. He ran a hand across his jaw and nodded.

If ever there was a time for a man to speak up, this was it.

He was fairly certain Miranda had no idea what was coming. She'd looked a little stunned when he said he had other plans for Christmas morning, and he hadn't been able to tell her otherwise.

He hadn't wanted to hurt her feelings, and he knew he had. He felt sorry about that. But he *did* have other plans, and hopefully, by the end of the day, any sorrow she had felt by his supposed rejection would turn to joy.

* * *

Miranda sat in front of the Christmas tree with Hudson on one knee and Harper on the other. They were tearing into their presents like nobody's business. Somehow even at nine months they seemed to grasp the gift-getting idea, although Hudson was more fascinated with the wrapping paper and the boxes than he was most of the presents she'd given him.

Harper liked the toys, especially the ones with lights and noises.

"You probably thought that baby drum set sounded like a good idea at the time," Charlotte said with a laugh, "but mark my words, you're going to be regretting that purchase in less than a day."

"Don't worry," Mason said with a shrug. "Hudson will break it in a week. That's how it goes during these first few years."

"I'm going to enjoy every second," Miranda assured them. "This is the best Christmas I've ever had. It's so much fun with children."

"Isn't it, though?" Charlotte agreed, pulling her own toddler into her lap.

Miranda sighed happily and leaned back on her hands. With all the presents open, she could just sit back and enjoy her twins. She wished Simon were here, though. He would have liked watching Hudson and Harper open their gifts. And he would have laughed when Hudson tried to stuff a wad of wrapping paper into his mouth.

She couldn't imagine where Simon could be on this Christmas morning, now that the youth group was delivering his dogs, but he'd said he had other plans. More likely he just wanted to spend a nice, quiet holiday alone, without all the fuss children would make. He loved the twins to death, but she suspected he'd had way more celebrating already this year than he was used to.

"I think there's one more present for the twins to open," Mason said, looking mysteriously around the room, "but I've forgotten where I put it. Hold on just a second. If I'm not mistaken, I think I left it in the spare room."

"Did you hear that, my sweethearts?" she asked the twins. "There's one more present for you. Yay!"

Miranda clapped, and Harper clapped with her. Hudson picked up the excitement, pumping his chubby arms and babbling eagerly.

"This is heavier than it looks."

A jolt of adrenaline shot through Miranda and her pulse leaped into overtime.

That wasn't Mason's voice coming from behind her—it was Simon's.

"Simon," she exclaimed, peeking over her shoulder to smile at him. "I thought you weren't going to make it."

"Yeah, well, I have a very special delivery to make. You didn't think I'd forget the twins, did you?"

He hefted a large foil-wrapped box onto the floor in front of Hudson and Harper.

"Here you go, kiddos. Rip off the paper to your heart's content."

"You were watching?"

Simon grinned.

"The whole thing. I've been standing in the hallway for near on an hour now. I about lost it when Hudson crammed the paper in his mouth."

"Why didn't you come on in here and join us?" Miranda asked, wondering why Mason and Charlotte hadn't considered the same thing. She felt like she was missing something.

Mason's face gave away nothing, but Charlotte's eyes were sparkling.

Simon crouched by the box, waiting for the big reveal.

"This is why I didn't bring their gift out until now," he said cryptically, his killer half smile making Miranda's stomach flip over.

The box was rocking back and forth so hard Miranda was afraid it might tip over onto its side.

"Hudson, go easy on the present. It might be breakable."

But Hudson wasn't pushing on the box. Neither was Harper.

"Simon?" she queried.

"Wait for it." He held up a hand. "Wait for it."

A moment later Zig and Zag came tumbling out of the box, a big green bow on Zig and a matching red one on Zag. The twins squealed in delight.

So did Miranda.

"I thought you said you'd adopted these two out," she said. "A special, private adoption, as I recall. Did the family back out on you?"

"The family," he said with a smile, "is sitting right here in this room."

"You kept them for *us*?"

"Now, before you say anything, I know you said you didn't want to have dogs in the house, but—"

Miranda leaped forward and flung herself into Simon's arms, bowling him over and knocking both of them to the floor.

"Easy, there, sweetheart," he said, his blue eyes glowing with affection.

"I'm just so happy. I had decided to ask you if we could adopt Zig and Zag, since the twins love them so much, but before I had the opportunity, you said they weren't available. I was so disappointed."

"I'm glad you like them."

"Like them? I love them."

And I love you, she wanted to say. But Mason

and Charlotte were in the room, and Simon was a very private person.

Today, though. Sometime. Maybe after dinner. She'd pull him aside and tell him how she felt about him. It was frightening, putting herself out there, but love was worth the possibility of being rejected.

And if he didn't feel the same way?

Well, she wouldn't make the relationship between them awkward, no matter what. He was Hudson and Harper's godfather, and the very best male role model they would ever have. She'd never take that away from him, or the twins.

But she hoped beyond hope that he would say he loved her, too.

She stood and stretched. Her legs had gone to sleep holding both babies on them simultaneously.

"Shall I set the table for dinner?" she asked Charlotte, who was laughing at one of her own children's antics as they all gathered around the overexcited Westies, who were wagging their tails so hard their entire back ends were moving.

"What? Oh, well, of course, later. But… I think there's another present that hasn't been opened yet."

Another one?

Nothing could *possibly* top Zig and Zag. They were the highlight of Christmas morning, one she would remember for the rest of her life. She hoped Charlotte wouldn't be too disappointed if the twins didn't show much interest in whatever new gift was about to be presented to them. She doubted they'd be interested in much of anything besides the dogs for the rest of the week, at least.

And then they'd grow up together. Hudson and Zig. Harper and Zag.

She reached down and scratched Zig's ear and he nuzzled her hand.

Cute little thing. She couldn't imagine how she ever thought she wasn't a dog person.

"I don't know why it's taken me so long to—"

She had been going to say she realized that she was indeed a dog person and couldn't imagine why she hadn't had a pet before now, but when she turned, it was to find Simon on one knee, a red velvet box in his hand.

And in the box…

She never finished that sentence about the dogs.

"Simon?"

Yes. Her answer was yes. He didn't even have to ask her the question.

But when she held her left hand out to him, he shook his head.

"Not yet. I've got this speech I wrote and memorized and I'm going to say it before I lose my nerve."

He'd written a *speech* for her?

And even more surprising, he was going to give it to her in front of Mason and Charlotte and all the kids?

She knew what it took for him to do that. And yet for her, he was pulling out all the stops, getting out of his comfort zone to impress her. The warmth in her heart was the most wonderful feeling she had ever experienced.

"Okay," she said, dropping her arm to her side. "Continue."

He cleared his throat.

"As you know, I've spent most of my life alone, living what was basically a completely solitary existence, with the exception of my dogs. And I was fine with that, up until the day I walked into a room and saw the most beautiful woman in the world stretched out underneath a made-up sheet tent, reading a fairy tale to my two favorite godchildren, loudly sipping a box of juice through a straw and munching on a cheese stick."

"Your only godchildren, I think," Mason said with a laugh.

"Hush, you," Charlotte warned. "This is so romantic. Don't ruin it. *You've* never written me a speech."

Mason snorted.

Simon was still gazing up at Miranda, his face turning as red as his shirt.

"I think we ought to let him finish," she suggested. If he felt anything like she did, breathing was an issue right now.

"I was really hard on you when you first came to town. But it didn't take me long to realize how dedicated you are to Hudson and Harper, how much you love them, and how much they love you. And along the way somewhere, I realized—"

He stopped and forced himself to breathe evenly a few times, inhale and exhale. Miranda was breathing right along with him, afraid if she didn't, she might pass out from the sheer excitement of it all.

A speech was great and all, especially from a man who usually never put more than two words together, but she was anxious to get to the part about the ring.

"I—I realized—"

He stopped again.

"I love you," she blurted, letting him off the hook. "I've never known a man with as much loyalty and honor as you have. And I so admire how much you love Hudson and Harper. I feel like I should pinch myself to make sure I'm really here and not just dreaming this."

Simon cringed. "Please don't do that."

He stood and reached for her left hand, slipping the diamond solitaire on her finger. It glinted in the light as she showed it off to Charlotte. She couldn't wait to take some pictures of it. Simon would have to deal with having her joy posted on social media, just this once.

"I forgot the rest of my speech."

She framed his face in her hands, relishing the feel of the shadow of his beard under her palms.

"You don't need a speech. I only want to hear three little words from you."

"Marry me, please?"

She laughed and kissed him.

"That wasn't quite what I had in mind."

"I'll try it again, then." He placed his hands over hers and brushed his lips over her mouth.

"I love you."

"That works for me."

"I love you."

"You said that already."

"I love you. And I'm just getting started here. I love you." He chuckled. "You're going to hear that every day for the rest of your life, probably several times a day, now that I've got the hang of it. I'm going to do everything in my power to be the best husband to you and the best father to the twins that I can be, with the Lord as my guide."

"Oh, Simon," she breathed as he kissed her again. Then she turned and picked up Hudson. "Did you hear that, little man? Uncle Simon is going to be your new daddy."

"And you, sweet miss," said Simon, swinging

Harper into the air and then kissing her cheek several times until she giggled, "aren't going to get to date until you're thirty. I never played baseball, but I have a bat."

"I say the same thing about my girls," Mason said approvingly.

"I'm so happy for you both," Charlotte exclaimed, embracing them in a big hug. "I've had a feeling about you two since the very beginning."

Miranda didn't know about the *very* beginning. Simon hadn't even liked her then. But she was looking forward to seeing what the future would hold for the four of them.

"Our forever family," she murmured.

Simon grinned and wrapped her and the twins in his big, strong arms, kissing each one of them in turn and lingering with Miranda.

"I like the sound of that," he whispered over her lips. "Our forever family."

* * * * *

If you enjoyed this story, try these books
by Deb Kastner!

THE COWBOY'S TWINS
MISTLETOE DADDY

Available now from Love Inspired!

***

And be sure to check out the other books
in the CHRISTMAS TWINS *series:*

AMISH CHRISTMAS TWINS
by Patricia Davids
and
SECRET CHRISTMAS TWINS
by Lee Tobin McClain

Find more great reads at
www.LoveInspired.com

Dear Reader,

Cowboys, twins, dogs and Christmas in Texas. Could there be a better or cuter combination?

Miranda Morgan has to change her whole lifestyle when she becomes the guardian of her sister's twins, but it's a change she's ready and willing to make. Unfortunately, the twins' godfather, Simon West, doesn't believe people can change, and he doesn't think Miranda is up to the task of becoming the twins' new mother.

Sometimes, even with the best of intentions, two people clash, and this is the case for Simon and Miranda. They both want what is best for the twins, but they have opposite notions of how to get things done. It's in learning to appreciate their differences that they can work together to accomplish their goals—and discover their dreams might not be so different after all.

If you enjoyed reading about Zig and Zag and the other dogs in *Texas Christmas Twins*, I encourage you to look into adopting a dog at your local shelter. There are so many great dogs looking for their Forever Family.

I'm always delighted to hear from you, dear readers, and I love to connect socially. You can find my website at www.debkastnerbooks.com. Come join me on Facebook at www.Facebook.

com/debkastnerbooks, and you can catch me on Twitter, @debkastner.

Please know that I pray for each and every one of you daily.

Love Courageously,
Deb Kastner

Get 2 Free Books,
Plus 2 Free Gifts—
just for trying the
Reader Service!